BOUND TOGETHER
BY SILENCE

"Here, I'll dial for you," Todd said.

He passed the phone to Cathy. Her heart was pounding.

"Hello?" A woman's voice this time.

Cathy took a deep breath. Her voice came out ragged and raspy. "Someone tried—to—kill—me."

Complete silence. For a moment she thought the connection was broken. Then the sound of breathing started, quick and in little gasps, like someone trying to get enough air. Todd stepped closer, moving the receiver away from her ear, so he could hear too. He pointed to the phone, then to Cathy. His lips formed the words, "Go on."

Her hands were moist and her mouth dry. "Someone tried to kill me," she gasped.

She was still holding the receiver so the others could hear, but it wasn't necessary. The next thing she knew, the telephone exploded.

"Mary Ann? Mary Ann! Oh, my God, where are you?"

Just Dial A Number

EDITH MAXWELL

AN ARCHWAY PAPERBACK
Published by POCKET BOOKS
New York   London   Toronto   Sydney   Tokyo   Singapore

An Archway Paperback published by
POCKET BOOKS, a division of Simon & Schuster Inc.
1230 Avenue of the Americas, New York, NY 10020

ISBN: 0-671-72867-9

First Pocket Books printing March 1972

30 29 28 27 26 25 24 23 22

AN ARCHWAY PAPERBACK and colophon are registered trademarks of Simon & Schuster Inc.

Printed in the U.S.A.

IL 7+

To Bobbe and Ben

Just Dial A Number

CHAPTER 1

It was at the final performance of *Murder at Midnight*, at the crucial moment, that something happened to the tape recorder. Cathy Shorer had just delivered her big line, her only line, in the show—"Someone tried to kill me . . ."—let the receiver drop from her hand, and had fallen, sinuously, weightlessly, to the floor . . . dead.

The lights dimmed the stage to a near blackout, but the strains of far-out, eerie music—which were to provide atmosphere, as Miss Evans, the director, explained—simply never came on. From where Cathy lay, she could see Miss Evans standing in the shadows off stage, her face a study in horror and shock. Then Todd Dillon, due on stage to discover the body, leaped instead to the tape recorder, his hands hopelessly tangling with Paul Gerow's. But still no music.

1

Suddenly Cathy wanted to giggle, partly from nervousness, partly from the sight of Miss Evans' face, but mostly from watching Todd and Paul, tackling the tape recorder like a football, trying to beat it into submission, which was impossible because, as she learned later, the tape had broken.

Cathy tried to lie still. After all, she was a corpse; but the moment stretched on and on in awkward, dark silence. The back of her hand felt like ants were crawling over it, and a little chill rippled up her spine. Weren't they ever going to fix the tape?

Then she watched Miss Evans grip the back of Todd's coat collar, disengage him from the tape, point him in the right direction, and propel him on stage with such force that he stumbled the first few steps, caught himself, rushed to Cathy and knelt beside her.

"What happened?" Cathy whispered.

"Shut up—you're dead," Todd whispered back.

And the show went on—without music.

Later, when the whole thing was over, curtain calls made, everyone was granted the mercy of open laughter. Everyone except Miss Evans, who took Paul Gerow aside and delivered a firm lecture on the basic fundamentals of a tape recorder, and how those backstage in charge of music were just as important as those on stage.

Paul spread his hands in innocence. "I didn't do a thing, Miss Evans. I could swear that tape decided to conk out on its own. Just to show us."

Finally, philosophically, Miss Evans gave a dear

2

little speech to the whole cast about the traditions of the theatre, how the show must go on, and how his experience might have taught them something useful for another time. Several of the cast mumbled something about there not being another time. Ever.

When she finished her talk, Paul Gerow, always the gentleman, invited Miss Evans to drop by the cast party at his house. But she said she'd had enough for one night and was going home. Most of the cast thought this was a good idea.

By the time Cathy and Todd got into his V.W. to drive to the party, it had begun to rain. They rolled up the windows, turned on the radio, and Cathy slid over next to Todd so their shoulders were touching. Cathy was exhilarated. Having been to hell and back again with the whole cast gave her a real "in" feeling. Things were always exciting around Todd. In fact, ever since she and Todd had been going together, the whole world had been painted in brighter colors.

When Todd's family moved into town six months ago, this fantastic hunk did not go unnoticed by anyone. His father, an Army colonel, had been an Assistant Army Attaché in London; his retirement brought Todd to California. Deedee Wyman, who had been to Europe on a tour last summer while her parents were getting a divorce, said that all British men looked to her as though they had dandruff. But Todd Dillon had neither dandruff nor was he British. This beautiful creature, who had

3

chosen Cathy Shorer from a long list of availables, wore tweed jackets, was comfortably tall, had dark hair with sideburns, Newman-blue eyes, and those sensitive lips that never quite close all the way.

Todd took one hand off the steering wheel and rubbed the back of his neck. "The way she pushed me onstage. My God, it was like being launched off a rocket pad! I never knew little ol' Evans could pack such a wallop."

The car swerved to the right.

"Hey, watch it," Cathy said.

"Anything you say, sweetheart." Todd replaced his left hand on the steering wheel, but then put his right arm around her shoulder.

She pushed him away. "You're a reckless driver, you know that, Todd Dillon? Keep your hands on the steering wheel where they belong."

"O.K., O.K. But the way you look tonight—"

"It's just my sexy greasepaint from the show."

"It's those fake eyelashes. I mean, they turn a guy on."

Cathy laughed.

It was raining harder by the time they reached Paul's house. Paul Gerow's home, located in the hills of their suburban town on the peninsula south of San Francisco, was built into the side of a bluff. The streets were narrow and winding, and by the time they arrived, the entire area in front of the house was choked with cars. Todd and Cathy ran through the rain to the door, shook their wet coats, hung them in the closet, and walked downstairs to the lower-level playroom.

The music from the record player was hot and loud. The crisis about the tape must have set the adrenaline running through everybody's veins, because the whole gang was still jazzed up, still talking about the show.

Deedee Wyman, who had played the heroine, walked around the room, still explaining to anyone who would listen. "After it happened, the whole thing seemed unreal. I said my lines, but without background music, they sounded so dumb."

"Forget it, let's dance." Paul grabbed Deedee's arm. Paul and Deedee had been going together for nearly a year. Paul was quiet and serious, Deedee a real crack-up. Opposites attract, everyone said.

Cathy and Todd mingled for a while, then danced. Paul's mother had fixed a big platter of sandwiches and filled the little bar refrigerator with soft drinks. Cathy glanced out the plate glass window. A solid sheet of water flowed from the overhang of the roof, so that the party inside might have been taking place on their own private submarine. It occurred to Cathy that this was one of those rare times of total happiness.

That is, until she went upstairs, headed for the little girls' room, and spied the group in the kitchen. She smelled the icky, sweet odor of marijuana immediately.

Jerry Miller screeched, "Cool it, the C.I.A.'s coming."

Several of the kids pretended to hide their joints, and someone giggled.

The crack about the C.I.A. meant her—Cathy Shorer. Because if her father caught any student at Arlington High smoking pot—on or off campus —there would be hell to pay. Since she was the Dean's daughter, they were afraid she might also be his spy. "Narc," they called a narcotics spy. She hated that word.

Cathy met their insolent stares, shrugged and forced herself to walk lightly and erect down the hall.

"Keep the faith, baby," Jerry called after her, and then laughed.

"What's so funny?" someone asked.

"Cathy's funny. Didn't she look funny to you?"

She closed the bathroom door to the sound of their laughter and leaned against the sink, biting her lip. They weren't laughing at her, personally. Not really. They said when you were high on grass, anything or anyone was funny. Even unfunny things were funny, so you just laughed.

But just like that, the good, warm, belonging feeling was gone. She was back in the limbo of being Dean Shorer's daughter—one of Them in age, but one of the Establishment by a blood tie too close for comfort; which left her suspended some place around dead center of the generation gap. Didn't they know they could smoke grass or do anything they wanted? She'd never cluck her tongue, and she'd certainly never tell. What if she went in there now and asked for a hit? No, then they'd really have something on her. She could see it now, all lit up like a movie marquee: "Dean Shorer's Daughter Busted for Smoking Grass." Then they'd really have the final, hilarious laugh.

Someone knocked on the door. "Anyone in there?" It was Deedee's voice.

"It's me. Come on in."

"Hi." Deedee took a comb from her purse and ran it through her long, blonde hair. Deedee Wyman was the kind of person you could talk to. Perhaps that was why she and Cathy were such good friends.

"They're smoking grass in there," Cathy said.

"Uh huh." Deedee continued to comb her hair with graceful unconcern.

"Deedee, when I walked by, Jerry Miller said, 'Here comes the C.I.A.'"

"That's on account of your father. They're afraid you'll tell."

"I wouldn't."

Deedee carefully smoothed her bangs. "Of course you wouldn't. But they don't know it."

"Sometimes I'm tempted . . . you know, to try it . . . to prove . . ."

Deedee's hand froze in mid-air. "Prove what? That you're not a nice, wholesome girl?"

Cathy swallowed hard. "Call me anything, Deedee, but don't call me wholesome."

Deedee grinned. "What's the matter, you got an identity crisis?"

"No, I'm just not—wholesome."

"O.K., you're stupid then. Listen, Cath, smoking grass is just for starters. Too many people graduate to something that gives them bigger kicks." She jammed her comb in her purse and slammed it shut. "You do what you want. But I'm not going to get started on anything, because I want to stay on top of things. I don't want things on top of me. Ever."

Having said her piece, Deedee left.

Cathy sighed, opened the door, and followed Deedee out.

The pot smokers had broken up and joined the party downstairs, bringing with them their own brand of joyous howling. Cathy searched for Todd. She finally spotted him leaning against the stone fireplace, talking to Allyson Troy. Allyson, seated on the raised ledge of the fireplace, threw back her head and laughed.

Allyson Troy had masses of thick, dark hair, which made a striking contrast to her delicate skin. But there was something about her eyes—under those extravagant, thick lashes. The glacial expression in them gave you the impression she had no soul.

It was difficult to get across the room, it was so noisy and crowded. There were a lot of crashers here tonight. As Cathy approached, Todd yelled over the music, "Hi! Where you been?"

Allyson looked up. "Hi," she said.

"Hi," Cathy replied.

Cathy had the feeling that if she and Allyson

Troy were stranded on a desert island for ten years, their conversation would never get past the "Hi" stage.

"Todd, I'm about to crash. Let's go, huh?"

She hated herself for being chicken like this. The name of the game was, of course, to stay and out-sparkle Allyson. But after what happened upstairs, and now Allyson, she suddenly felt so bushed, so totally bushed, just trying to keep a smile on her face was work.

Todd was all jazzed. "Allyson wants us to come over to her house for a swim. Her parents are in Hawaii. There's just the housekeeper there, so we can have our own private little party—you and me, Allyson and Jerry Miller."

Allyson allowed a hint of a smile to touch her lips.

Cathy wanted to say, "You have everything, Allyson—big house, swimming pool, fantastic eye-lashes. You'd like to add Todd to the list too, wouldn't you?" She was always thinking of things like that, things she'd never say, because she had to keep her cool.

"Lose your cool, kid, and you lose Todd." She ought to print that on a sign—in old English letter-ing, maybe—and tape it to the mirror over her dressing table.

"Allyson says their pool's still heated." Todd was urging. "Would you believe a swim in the rain?"

Cathy shivered. "Well, it sounds like fun, but I've sort of got a headache."

Todd glanced around. "We've got to get out of here, anyway. God, those kids are high. If Paul's parents show up, we're all in trouble."

Paul was hustling around, getting rid of the howlers.

"Todd, don't you think you ought to help Paul?" Cathy asked. "His parents might come home any minute."

"He can handle it," Todd shrugged. "This party is going to self-destruct in about five minutes anyway."

Allyson spoke then. "Those kids are such infants. If a person wants to smoke pot, he should do it . . . well, discreetly."

Discreetly meant at Allyson's house, with Jerry Miller. Jerry could have more fun, calling Cathy the "C.I.A." He'd probably even think of a better one by the time they got to Allyson's.

"How about it? You kids coming?" Allyson addressed Todd.

"We'll see," Todd said, taking Cathy's arm. While his words were casual, his parting glance conveyed the message that he, at least, would see Allyson later.

Todd juggled her through the crowd. When they were upstairs Cathy said, "I don't think I'd better go, Todd."

"Why not?"

"I just don't want to. Why don't we go to my house instead?"

He made a fist and slid it gently across her chin.

"Hey, you're not worried about Allyson, are you? Cath . . . you jealous?"

"No." She shook her head. "It's just this . . . splitting headache." Why, for heaven's sake, couldn't she think of a less Victorian excuse. A headache!

Todd said nothing and they walked to the car in silence. He jammed the V.W. in gear and they started down the hilly, rainswept road. "Look," she said finally. "I know you like to go where the action is. Me too. It's just—"

He didn't answer.

"Todd, have you ever smoked grass?"

After a long pause, he said, "Oh. So that's the deal? Listen, Cath, you don't have to smoke grass or do anything you don't want to. I mean, it's a free country. But live a little, huh?"

She was so tired. Too tired to argue, or even answer him. Ever since she fell in love with Todd she felt she had to be the *most* in the looks department, the clothes department, and the personality department. The personaliy department. That's what filled her to the brim with fatigue. That's what made her dream of lying in a grassy meadow in the sun some place—some place she'd seen once as a child—probably back in Virginia, visiting her grandparents.

Todd shrugged. "O.K., I'll take you home."

By the time they pulled up in front of her house the rain had let up a bit Todd left the keys in the ignition and walked her to the door.

11

"You sure you don't want to come in?" she asked pointlessly.

"No. Not if you've got a headache. Tomorrow maybe."

"Good. I'll call Deedee and Paul and we'll all get together over here."

But he was already walking down the front steps, without even kissing her good night. "I'll call you tomorrow." He waved as his car swooped away from the curb.

She knew he was going to Allyson's. He was disappointed in her too. The business about the headache had been stupid. What she really meant was, "I can't stand Allyson, and I can't stand Jerry Miller. People like that get me uptight and I lose my cool. And I don't want you to see me in a poor light, Todd. I just can't afford it."

CHAPTER 2

It was still raining the next night. But Cathy brought in extra logs for the fireplace before the others arrived, so the fire would be bright and hot. Like the conversation, she hoped. Twenty-four hours had made a lot of difference. Cathy felt better tonight, more comfortable because she would be playing in her own backyard with her friends, Deedee and Paul. She pretended the pink sweater and pink plaid pants she was wearing were a suit of magic armor, as if, by their color alone, Todd would see her in a rosy light.

Deedee and Paul came early. Todd didn't show up until after nine. He never mentioned going to Allyson's and Cathy had sense enough not to ask. At first he seemed pretty uptight. But his eyes followed Cathy as she moved about the room and sometimes he laughed when she thought of clever

13

things to say. Maybe it was going to be a successful evening after all.

Paul sat on the floor in front of the fire.

"Your party was some blast." Deedee stretched out, putting her head in his lap.

"Yeah, once I got rid of the pot smokers," Paul replied.

"Had they left by the time your parents got home?" Cathy asked.

"Most of them. We had a few stragglers."

Deedee sat up. "Oh, Paul, what did your parents think?"

"That they were drunk."

"Just drunk?" Todd was incredulous.

"Yeah, I opened the windows and aired the place out—not that my parents would have known what pot smells like anyway. My father got real fired up though. He said, 'No beer allowed on the premises.' I guess that's what they did when he was young—drink beer."

"Well, I suppose what they don't know won't hurt them," Cathy remarked. "I don't mean that sarcastically, Paul. I really don't. Because if your parents did know, it would only—"

Paul nodded. "Yeah, I guess they're pretty naïve, considering—"

Considering Paul's older brother, Jacques, was a real hippie-weirdo, Cathy thought to herself. Maybe that's what made Paul so straight, such a thoroughly nice guy, so thoughtful of his parents. Perhaps he was trying to make up for Jacques. Or had Paul

14

been born that way, and Jacques born the bad seed? Who knew?

Afraid things were getting too serious, Cathy put on another stack of records, turned up the volume, and sat back on the stacked cushions on the floor. "Todd, I'll never forget the look on your face when Miss Evans pushed you on stage. You were too much!"

Paul joined in. "Talk about stumbling onto a corpse. Man, you nearly walked on top of her."

Todd laughed. "And when I got to her, she was still yakking, asking what happened. I mean, this is one chick who can't keep quiet, even when she's supposed to be dead."

"I always talk too much when I'm around you," Cathy observed. There was more truth to the statement than she cared to admit, even to herself.

Todd, who could never sit still, stood up and began to pace the floor. "Admit it," he quoted from the play. "Admit you took her life."

"Inspector, you can't mean—" Deedee slapped her brow and rolled her eyes. She was mimicking Allyson's part in the show.

Todd stopped pacing. "Allyson kept her cool, though. After the music went off, she never missed a beat."

"Good for her," Cathy said, a little louder than she intended. She immediately regretted it.

Todd snapped, "Allyson's a real cool chick."

"Who said she wasn't?" A small flame of defiance burned within Cathy.

Something changed the minute Allyson's name came up. There was a tension in the room. Or was Cathy imagining things? Of course Todd had gone to Allyson's last night. Had Jerry Miller shown up too? She hoped so. But what happened? Had they gone skinny-dipping in her pool? Or were those stories just gossip?

Cathy spread the cushions on the floor, flopped down on her stomach, and glanced sideways at Todd. She wiggled to a more comfortable position, aware that Todd was watching her. The knowledge gave her the weirdest feeling of hotness—her whole backside seemed burning, and the sensation must have shown itself in her face, for now Todd was staring at her as if he were bewitched.

Displaying herself successfully in the pink outfit cheered Cathy; it stirred up a stronger defiance.

"Allyson's really cool," Cathy repeated for emphasis.

"She's okay——" Todd broke off abruptly and for an instant his unfinished sentence seemed to hang in the air. Then slowly, thoughtfully, Todd raised his hand in a salute. It was as if he'd said to Cathy, "But you're the best." His slight gesture had a meaning plainer than words.

Paul must have noticed the little scene because he grinned, tossed Deedee off his lap, stood up and yawned. "Enough slapstick." His words were directed toward Cathy, and for a moment she and Paul seemed to share their own private joke.

As though it were catching, Deedee too yawned.

She shook her long, blonde hair. "It's nearly ten. I've got to go home."

"You kids can't go." Cathy was exhilarated. "Todd's given us his lines, but I haven't had chance to rehash my line."

"Your beautiful death scene, you mean?" Todd guffawed. "Cathy has one line. One single line in the whole show and from then on she's a corpse!"

"But what a line!" Cathy stood up, swept to the desk and picked up the phone.

"Someone tried to kill me," Todd mocked in a false soprano.

"Be quiet, Todd," she said. "It went like this. 'Someone tried to kill me.'" She held the button on the phone down and repeated her only line in the show.

"Once more with feeling, Sarah Heartburn," Todd cheered her on.

"Someone tried to kill me." She was really hamming it up now.

Todd slapped his leg and laughed.

"Ping!" Paul snapped his fingers. "Tape breaks. Evans panics. Todd panics. I panic. Evans throws Todd on stage. Corpse laughs visibly, but the show goes on!"

"I was not laughing visibly, Paul. I never moved a muscle."

"So you never moved a muscle. Give the little lady an Oscar for never moving a muscle, so Deedee and I can go home," Paul said.

Then Todd had an idea. "Listen, gang. I'll bet

17

Cath could call someone right now, give 'em her line, and really shake them up."

Deedee laughed. "Not a chance."

Paul said, "You're bad, Cathy-baby, but not that bad. They might believe you, so I wouldn't try."

"Of course they'd believe me. That's why I wouldn't try it."

"You'd probably crack up in the middle of the line anyway, Sarah Heartburn," Todd laughed.

"I would not."

"Not—what?" Todd grabbed her, cupping her chin in his hand.

"I would not crack up," Cathy repeated.

"Wanna bet?" Todd was warming up to the idea. "O.K., Sarah. Call someone, give 'em your line, and see what happens."

"Not one of the kids in the show," Deedee piped up. "They'd remember the line."

"Skip it," Paul said.

Cathy paused.

"Maybe you kids are right. Sarah Heartburn couldn't fool anyone." There was a note of challenge in Todd's voice.

Cathy gave a shake of her head. "First you say I could, then you say I couldn't. You just watch!" She picked up the receiver and started to dial.

"What if it's not a real number?" Deedee looked nervous.

"Everybody in town has the same first two digits. So dial them—then just improvise," Todd said, chuckling.

18

"Quiet," Cathy whispered. The dial tone clicked off, then the phone was ringing on the other end of the line.

"Hello?" It was a child's voice. Cathy hung up, relieved.

Todd was amused. "What's the matter? Stage fright?"

"No, it was a little kid. I tried though, and you said I wouldn't."

"So try again," Todd said. "Here, I'll dial for you."

Paul groaned. "You kids are nuts. I've got to go home. You ready, Deedee?"

Todd raised his hand. "Wait, it's ringing now." He passed the phone to Cathy. Her heart was pounding.

"Hello?" A woman's voice this time.

Cathy took a deep breath. Her voice came out ragged and raspy. "Someone tried—to—kill—me."

Complete silence. For a moment she thought the connection was broken. Then the sound of breathing started, quick and in little gasps, like someone trying to get enough air. Todd stepped closer, moving the receiver away from her ear, so he could hear too. He pointed to the phone, then to Cathy. His lips formed the words, "Go on."

Her hands were moist and her mouth dry. "Someone tried to kill me," she gasped.

She was still holding the receiver so the others could hear, but it wasn't necessary. The next thing she knew, the telephone exploded.

19

"Mary Ann? Mary Ann! Oh, my God, where are you?"

Cathy's stomach turned over, and she dropped the receiver on the desk with a crash. Backing away, she shuddered and looked at the phone—as though it were alive.

Todd reached over and put the receiver back on the hook.

Paul let out a low whistle. "Wow! You scared the hell out of someone."

Nobody spoke for a moment, then Todd laughed half-heartedly. "Aw, the woman will know it's a joke."

"Yeah? And what if she doesn't?" Paul asked dryly.

"Well, gee, maybe you ought to call her back," Deedee suggested.

Paul kept staring at the phone. "Call who back? Todd doesn't even know who he dialed."

"That's right, I don't," Todd said blankly.

They stood, looking at one another. It was so quiet it was eerie, and the ticking of the grandfather clock in the front hall sounded terribly loud— like time was passing, and what were they going to do about it.

Todd's voice broke the silence. "Aw, come on you kids. Whoever answered the phone will know it's a joke—or find it out real fast. Mary Ann . . . some name! Sounds like a real ding-a-ling."

Deedee started for the door. "Coming, Paul?"

"Yeah, let's go."

Todd saluted Cathy. "Great performance, Sarah. Maybe you'll get two lines in the next play." Halfway to the door, he turned. "Mind if I stick around for a minute?"

"I don't mind," she said. Though in a way she did. Suddenly, for no reason, she wanted to be alone. She had that awful, tired feeling again.

Todd collapsed on the sofa while she carried the empty coke bottles to the kitchen and cleaned up. She turned off the kitchen light, but instead of returning to the living room, she stood in the dark, staring out the window into the fog which had come up since it stopped raining, listening to the planes flying low over the house, as they always did in bad weather.

She heard Todd's footsteps behind her and felt his arms encircle her waist. "You're some crack-up, you know that?" He nuzzled his face in her hair. "Let's go back in the living room where it's more comfortable."

But she kept staring out the kitchen window. "I did a dumb thing tonight, making that phone call."

"Forget it." He kissed the back of her neck.

"You're right, Todd. I do act like a Sarah Heartburn."

"Honest, I like you that way. You're crazy as hell."

"Is that why you like me? 'Cause I'm crazy?" she asked.

"Come in the living room and I'll show you why."

But she didn't move. "Todd, tell me something.

21

That first night we met—why did you ask me for a date the next night? Was there any one particular thing about me?"

"You were the Dean's daughter. And I needed another recommendation for West Point."

"Todd, be serious."

He pulled her toward the living room. "Let's be serious in there, in front of the fire."

"No, wait. Do you really like me, Todd?"

"I like you."

"Don't say it like that."

"How else can I say it? I like you. Everyone knows I like you. We've been nominated for Couple of the Year at school, haven't we?"

"But that's a contest. I mean, for real."

"So it's for real." He let go of her. "Oh, come off it, Cath. You females are all alike. You get a little action going—a little fun—then you turn serious, and all you want to do is yak!"

She followed him into the living room. "Todd—"

"Stop talking, will you?" He pulled her to the sofa, kissed her neck, then her cheek. A log in the fireplace broke, sending little red sparks up the chimney. His kiss sent little red sparks all over her.

Then her father's footsteps sounded on the stairs, and Todd jumped up.

"Good evening, Todd." Her father flicked on the light. He was wearing his old blue bathrobe and horrible tan slippers.

"Hello . . . sir." Todd threw back his shoulders.

"On my way to the refrigerator," her father explained pleasantly. "I'm an inveterate nighttime eater, you know. Have been for years."

"Yes, sir," Todd said, glancing at his watch. "I was just . . . running along." He backed out of the room.

After a quick, furtive kiss on the porch, Todd left. Cathy came into the house and headed for the kitchen. She leaned against the sink and folded her arms across her chest. "You are not an inveterate nighttime eater, and you know it, Dad."

"I came in for lemon pie," he replied.

"In that bathrobe? Honestly, Dad, it's embarrassing."

"What? My bathrobe? Or my inopportune entrance?"

She flushed. "You're too much. I'm going to bed."

"Yes. Well, good night then." Her father was peering into the refrigerator.

She was so tired she didn't even wash her face before going to bed. Tired and letdown and, most strange of all, not really angry with her father. She'd acted infantile tonight. She was always doing dumb things around Todd, things to make him notice her. Like if she didn't, he'd find someone else to notice. Allyson Troy, for instance.

She crawled into bed and lay there, staring at nothing. She heard her father come back upstairs. She flipped over on her stomach and pulled the pillow over her head. The ticking of the grandfather clock downstairs was so loud. Funny, it never bothered her before. She got up, closed the hall door, and her bedroom door. That was better.

Those planes roaring through the fog over the house sounded too close, as if they might skim the roof off. Why didn't they close the airport in weather like this?

In her mind she kept hearing that woman screaming over the phone. What a cruel thing, to scare someone like that. Whoever the woman was, Cathy hoped she'd forgive her.

CHAPTER 3

When she awoke, the queasy feeling of the night before was gone. It was just another Monday morning. Only today the sun was shining, like a California travel poster. Cathy came down to breakfast to find her father standing in the middle of the kitchen reading the morning paper, her mother pouring batter into the waffle iron.

She and her mother went into their usual routine. "I'll just have a bowl of cereal, Mom."

"You'll have a good hot breakfast."

"I'm late—"

Her mother opened the steaming waffle iron, exposing a sheet of yellow paste. She popped it shut. "Now it's going to stick."

"That's O.K. I don't feel like waffles anyway."

"I don't care. You can't go off on an empty stomach."

Her father glanced at them. "Put it to music, girls. Add a little soft shoe—"

Finally, Cathy and her mother wound up with a compromise: cereal and toast.

Cathy was pouring milk on her cereal when her father got around to the subject of last night. "You know, Cathy, ever since you met this Todd Dillon you've been acting—"

"I know—'like water jumping around a hot frying pan.' You said that before, Dad."

"Well, can you think of a more accurate description?"

"Yes," she said dreamily. "I've been choosed."

The word "choosed" was their private joke, dating back to the year she was in kindergarten and had rushed home that first Christmas to announce to her parents, "Guess what? I've been choosed to play Mary in the Christmas pageant." And her father, with his Ph.D. in English, had added the word "choosed" to his vocabulary with delight. They'd used it ever since.

Her father sat down at the table. "You were choosed by that boy, what's-his-name, last year. Don't forget that," he reminded her.

That boy had invited her to the Junior Prom because, as her father pointed out, he was already in trouble about the stolen car, and dating the Dean's daughter might give him a scintilla of respectability. Her father was big with words—like scintilla. She had to be careful not to let words like

26

that rub off and creep into her everyday conversation. When it happened, people gave her a funny stare.

"Cathy Shorer is the only kid in town who's trying to decrease her vocabulary," Deedee often remarked.

Cathy broke off a piece of toast. "That boy last year was a blatant opportunist, and I never considered dating him," she said, trying to beat her father at his own game.

"O.K., Cathy. But about this Todd character, just play it cool," her father answered, playing her game now.

Her father retreated behind the morning paper, her mother fiddled with the waffle iron, and Cathy sat, without further words, buttering her toast. The butter spread out, golden, like happiness. Happiness has been the past six months, she thought, going steady with Todd.

Yet, when she first met Todd, she didn't think she was going to like him. It was at a big blast at Deedee's house last fall. Cathy had wandered out of the living room and into the entrance hall. Todd Dillon was sitting in the little study off the hall, thumbing through *Road and Track*, looking as though he didn't have anything better to do. He did. There was a whole party going on in the next room.

Todd closed the magazine and looked up. "Hey, sweetheart, whatcha' doing out there? Come on in."

Cathy stood in the door and gestured toward the next room. "You bored or something?"

He ignored her question. "Sit down. I'm Todd Dillon."

She knew who Todd Dillon was all right—the big sensation who'd just moved to town.

"I'm Cathy Shorer," she replied. "I'd better be getting back . . . and getting . . ." People like Todd Dillon made her feel dumb, so that she found herself not completing sentences.

"What's the rush?" His smile was slow and easy.

That's when she thought she wasn't going to like Todd. She knew his type- -so sure of himself, that something he must have been born with which, even in strange surroundings, he never lost. The sureness which enabled him to sit out here in the study like this, away from the crowd, until something or someone interesting showed up.

And Todd was looking at her with interest.

"Did you—ah, come with somebody tonight?" he asked.

"Yes. Well, no, not actually." Actually, she'd come with two other girls. The boy she'd been going with had moved to New York that summer, and since then she'd had a few dates for a few parties, and no dates for a lot of parties.

"Well, let's join the action, then," Todd said, taking her hand. "Hey, what did you say your name was?"

"Cathy Shorer."

"Any relation to Dean Shorer?"

"He's my father," she said, watching for a reaction. But there was none. Neither good nor bad. That's when she began to like Todd Dillon.

He took her home that night. He asked her out the next night, and the night after that. Being "choosed" by Todd must have impressed a lot of others, too. She was asked to be a Pom Pom girl; and she and Todd had been nominated for Couple of the Year. Even her face, which at best was an in-between, nothing remarkable face, had acquired a sort of aura. Sometimes, with her long, chestnut dark hair just right, she stepped back from the mirror, squinted, and she looked—special, actually pretty.

Her mother said that since she'd been going with Todd she'd "really blossomed."

Deedee expressed it differently. "You've freaked out, kid."

Cathy had another name for it. It was love.

Love was a hearts-and-flowers word, a word she and Todd had never used. Yet, in spite of all its ups and downs—it was love. Even though her father had interrupted at the wrong moment last night, the evening had ended on a definite "up."

By the time Cathy left the house that morning she felt bright and sparkly, just like the weather. It occurred to her later that she had no inkling, not the slightest premonition, that the roof was about to cave in. It caved gradually, in little chunks.

The first hint of something wrong came at the beginning of the second period. She was changing into her gym clothes in the girls' dressing room when she overheard two girls, on the other side of the lockers, speaking in hushed tones.

"But it wasn't Mary Ann on the phone at all. Her mother just thought it was. See?"

"Then who was it?"

"Just somebody playing a joke, I guess."

"Some joke!"

The door slammed shut, cutting off their voices.

Cathy's gym blouse was halfway over her head, and for a moment her hands froze. She stood, like a statue, all tangled up in the white gym blouse. She felt the blood rush to her face. She knew she'd done a stupid thing last night. She knew the minute she heard that woman scream. What in the world had happened?

The bell rang, and she ran to gym class. She looked around. Who were the girls she'd overheard? Their voices were not familiar.

She forgot about it after that, at least consciously. She didn't actually forget. She chalked it up to experience . . . an experience she'd never repeat. So, by noon, when she came through the cafeteria line and spied Todd, Deedee, and Paul waiting at the usual corner table, and saw their drawn faces, she was honestly mystified.

"What's the matter?" She slipped into the chair next to Todd.

There was an odd silence.

"Oh, Cathy, something terrible's happened," Deedee whispered, not looking at her.

"What is it?"

Paul folded his paper napkin in squares, until it got the size of a postage stamp and he couldn't fold it any further. Then he looked up. "About this Mary Ann. Her name's Mary Ann Connolly. She's a sophomore here at Arlington."

"What's happened?" Cathy's jaw felt tight.

Paul's voice was hesitant. "Look, Cath, it was her mother you got on the phone. Her mother must have really thought you were Mary Ann. Because she and her husband got in the car and started home to Mary Ann."

"Started *home?*"

"They were at her grandmother's. They must have blown their minds, Cath. They told the grandmother to phone the police, and tore off in their car."

Suddenly, she didn't want to hear any more.

The hot lunch that day was corned beef and cabbage. She know later she'd always remember that moment and how she wanted to get up and run away from the smell of cabbage and the sight of Paul, Todd, and Deedee, from the white, remote expression on their faces. She wanted to escape before any of them could say another word.

But she remained seated, waiting, while Paul struggled with his words. "They had a bad accident."

Nobody said anything then. She thought she ought to ask Paul how bad the accident was, but found she didn't want to know. From the looks on their faces, she already knew. And all she could think of was, "Dear God, please don't let them say it."

It was Deedee who finally came out with it. "Oh, Cathy, they were killed. Both her parents were killed."

She tried to believe she wasn't crazy.

After a while she became aware of Todd's hand, gripping her wrist hard. His voice sounded far off.

"Look, Cathy, nobody knows. Just the four of us, and nobody's going to tell. What happened was an accident. I mean, it wasn't *your fault* they cracked up."

"But, Todd, what if they find out?" Deedee interrupted.

"How are they going to find out? There's no way. Listen, no one could connect Cathy with this Mary Ann."

"Yes, they could," Deedee said. "The line, 'Someone tried to'—well, you know. That was Cathy's line in the show."

"Oh, come off it," Todd thundered. "How many people heard that line? Two hundred? Three hundred? It's not Cathy's—"

"I know. But someone might associate it with Cathy," Deedee insisted.

"So? What does that prove?"

"It doesn't *prove* anything, but it might make someone suspicious."

"That's why we have to play it cool and keep our heads. No crime's been committed, Deedee. Nobody could prove anything. Besides, none of us even know her—"

"I do," Deedee said. "I know Mary Ann. She was in my art class last term. She's real talented."

"Big deal. That doesn't mean a thing." Todd leaned forward, lowering his voice. "Cathy had a monster-size piece of bad luck when she dialed that number. But that's what it was--Bad Luck."

"*Cathy* dialed the number?" Paul asked quietly.

Todd flushed. He stood up. "It doesn't matter who dialed the number. We're going to keep our mouths shut, that's what matters." He picked up his books.

"See you all later at the Malt Shop," he said over his shoulder as he left.

Cathy kept her eyes focused on her lap because she thought that might be the best way to keep from being sick. Finally she found her voice, and she was surprised because it was so calm.

"Do you kids believe what Todd said about it not being my fault?"

"Of course, we do," Deedee answered quickly. "For heaven's sake, they might have had an accident anyway—"

"Do you believe it, Paul?" she asked in the same calm voice.

He ran his hand through his hair. "I don't know, Cathy. What's done is done. None of us meant for it to happen."

The bell rang then and a hundred chairs scraped against the floor. She didn't think she could stand up. "I . . . I guess I'd better go home."

"Don't you dare!" Deedee whispered.

Paul tried to smile. "Take it easy, Cath. Deedee's right. You shouldn't leave. Look, we'll see you after school. We'll talk about it then, O.K.?"

"We can't!" Deedee said. "There's a meeting of the Pom Pom girls after school. Cathy and I have to go. It might look funny if we didn't."

It was then that Cathy wanted to laugh. She felt giddy, lightheaded. Paul's and Deedee's faces looked blurred, as though she were seeing them through a tank of water. She clasped her hand across her mouth in case she did laugh. Somehow, Deedee talking about a Pom Pom meeting seemed insanely funny, and she was afraid if she started laughing she'd never stop. Never.

She made it through the afternoon, the reason being that she had no other choice. But the minute school was out she headed straight for home, because she couldn't bear the thought of seeing Pom Pom girls . . . or anyone else.

Of course, Deedee was right. Someone was bound to put two and two together and come up with her name for an answer. When they did, she'd crack like one of her mother's Haviland cups. Therefore, it was important to go home, because she needed time to get ready.

Once home, she headed straight upstairs to her room, closed the door, and leaned back against it. The flowered bedspread, the white organdy curtains, the old red leatherbound dictionary on her desk— they all looked safe and familiar, and she found she wanted to reach out and touch them.

Later, she tried to sit down and think. But she was so cold she shivered, so she had to keep walking, moving, hugging herself with her arms. Even her brain seemed frozen, making it hard to think straight. She dug out her heavy ski sweater and slipped it on. But it didn't help much. The awful cold seemed to come from within.

Nothing added up. She tried to concentrate. What had Paul said? "They got in the car and started home to Mary Ann." Why the car? Why hadn't they just called home instead? She kept trying to put the story together. In the back of her mind she knew she'd done something too awful to think about, so it was better if she concentrated on figuring out the details.

The paper boy had the kind of car you could hear a block away. At the first sound, she ran for the stairs, and was waiting outside by the time the afternoon paper hit the front steps. Back in her room, she spread it out on the bed.

There, in cold black and white, were the missing details. Then, for the first time, she began to comprehend.

COUPLE KILLED AFTER
BOGUS PHONE CALL

A prank phone call resulted in the death of Mr. and Mrs. Frank Connolly of 53 Peach Street in a one-car accident on Whiteside Freeway about 10:00 P.M. yesterday.

Connolly's car apparently went out of control at the 28th Street underpass. Attending officers stated that excessive speed was the probable cause of the accident.

The couple was en route to their Peach Street address, according to Mrs. Eileen Connolly, mother of Frank Connolly. She told a *Times* reporter that her son and his wife had just left her apartment on State Street, following the bogus phone call indicating their daughter was in danger. The prankster then immediately hung up. Efforts to reach their daughter failed when the Connolly residence gave a busy signal. The parents left for home in their car immediately. After notifying police, Mrs. Eileen Connolly had the operator check the line and found the victims' daughter, Mary Ann, 15, unaware that anything was amiss, using the phone. . . .

Cathy couldn't read any further. Her head fell forward, hitting the newspaper with a crackle.

Out of all the people in this town, how could she

have called that particular number at that particular time? But she had. *She* had done it. Her innocent little joke, her showing off in front of Todd and the others, had caused the death of two people. A sickening picture crossed her mind. Two people . . . the car . . . the concrete wall at the underpass.

Some place downstairs she heard her mother calling, but she was too weak to answer. A few minutes later the bedroom door opened and her mother stepped in.

"Todd's on the phone," she said. "Why, Cathy, what's the matter? You're pale as a ghost!"

"Nothing," she lied.

That was her first lie, and she knew that everything after that was going to be a lie. Even downstairs, answering the phone, her voice was a lie.

"Todd?" she said casually, in an everyday tone.

"Cath, did you see the paper?"

"Yes."

"You're clear!"

"I'm . . . what?"

"You're clear. Didn't you read it? The paper said, 'indicating their daughter was in danger.' Not . . . that other thing."

"Oh."

"Didn't you notice?"

"No."

"The way I figure it is this. Mrs. ———," he paused, not wanting to use names, she guessed. "The lady, she repeated what she heard to her mother-in-law, and the mother-in-law repeated it to the reporters. And somehow, what you said, got lost in the translation. See?"

"I see," she answered dully.

"So that lets you off the hook." He let out a big sigh. "The way it stands now, the only person who actually *heard* you is . . . well, I mean she can't . . ."

"Todd, I'll call you back." She hung up because she knew she couldn't stand up much longer.

"You're clear, off the hook," he'd said. Her words got lost in the translation, so that let her off the hook. Todd too. That's why he was so relieved.

She should feel relief. She was safe. She should be jumping up and down with joy—or something. But she wasn't. Getting off the hook made surprisingly little difference, somehow. Because, as long as she lived, she'd carry the knowledge about herself in her mind. It would never be gone.

The bedspread, dictionary—everything in her room looked different. Nothing, she knew, would ever look the same again.

She sat on the bed, trying to decide what to do next—tomorrow, the day after, the rest of her life. She'd just keep on lying, she supposed.

CHAPTER 4

The following afternoon, when Cathy and Todd posed for Couple of the Year campaign photographs, even the camera lied. When Cathy saw the pictures later, there she stood with Todd's arms around her, her head thrown back, an incredibly carefree smile on her face.

The campaigning preceding the contest for Couple of the Year was a big deal for seniors at Arlington. The five couples who had been nominated were all wearing their best clothes and best smiles that afternoon.

Deedee and Paul met them afterward and the four of them headed for the school parking lot where Todd kept his V.W. They were on their way to the Malt Shop. As they walked across the gravel, Deedee seemed strangely silent. Cathy stared at her.

Deedee's face was almost as pale as her white leather jacket.

Deedee and Paul climbed into the back seat; Cathy slipped in front beside Todd.

Deedee leaned forward, propping her elbows on the front seat. "Todd, let's not go right away, huh? I've got something to tell you kids. And we can't really talk at the Malt Shop."

Todd swung his arm over the seat. "What's on your mind?"

"Well," Deedee stammered. "I mean, I've just got to tell *somebody*."

"What's the matter?" Paul was instantly alert.

Deedee cleared her throat and took a deep breath. "This afternoon I was talking to Marty Ruebeck. You know, the Ruebecks were good friends of the Connollys."

"Go on," Todd said cautiously.

"Marty told me that after the accident, the police took Mary Ann to her grandmother's apartment. Her grandmother's a nurse, you know. Anyway, about one o'clock in the morning, Mrs. Connolly called the Ruebecks, absolutely out of her mind. Mary Ann had disappeared! Marty's father got dressed and went over to Mrs. Connolly's. They called the police. Well, to make a long story short, the police found Mary Ann in the park, wandering around, all alone. At three in the morning! They brought her back to Mrs. Connolly's and called the doctor. The doctor said Mary Ann was suffering from shock, and gave her a shot to knock her out."

Cathy gave way to the curiously reeling sensation of being a speck of dust, utterly unable to stop Deedee from talking, or to keep herself from listening.

"Deedee, what's the point of this story?" Todd's voice was icy.

Deedee toyed with the ring on her finger. "There is no point, exactly. I mean, that's the whole story. I just . . . well, when Marty told me, I changed the subject right away, naturally. But I've been thinking about it ever since. It's been bugging me. I *had* to tell somebody . . . and you're the only ones . . ."

Cathy let out a little whimper. Todd reached for her hand, but Cathy pulled away.

Todd turned on Deedee. "Oh, cripes, Deedee! Just make sure you fill us in on all the gory details. Don't miss a one!"

"Shut up, Todd," Paul said.

Todd spread his hands to the heavens. "What's the matter with you kids anyway? I'm just trying to pick up the pieces of what's already a dirty mess —so it doesn't get any worse, doesn't go any further. And you jump on me like a pack of hungry wolves!"

"Well, skip it then," Paul snapped. "All this yak only makes it worse for Cathy and everybody. The way I look at it, we've hashed it over enough."

"I'm sorry," Deedee cried.

Todd gripped the steering wheel. "Let's forget it, huh? Could we please, possibly, just forget it?"

Cathy turned away. "How?" she said.

Silence made her turn back. "Todd, please just take me home," she whispered.

Paul stared out the window. "Let's all go. I'm going to walk."

"I'll come with you," Deedee said.

You could feel the relief in the air as Deedee and Paul got out of the car. It was, Cathy thought, as though the four of them were members of a secret society. No one else could join; but worst of all, none of them could get out.

When Todd let her off, Cathy said, "Thanks, Todd. I'll see you tomorrow." She noted that she sounded quite natural.

She hung her coat in the downstairs closet. She could hear her mother in the kitchen. Her father must be in the den, because she caught a whiff of his pipe smoke. She needed to get away, to be by herself for a while. She could go upstairs, take a hot bath. With water running in the tub no one could hear her crying. She filled the tub, poured in a capful of bubble bath, and slid under the white foam. But she did not cry.

It must have been cold, walking alone in the park at three in the morning. Foggy, too. What had the police said when they saw Mary Ann Connolly. "Hey, you! What do you think you're doing? What's your name?" Had she come home peacefully? The doctor gave her a shot. That was merciful. Dear God, that must have helped.

If she could only get the picture out of her mind.

She stepped from the tub, pulled the towel from the rack and dried herself vigorously.

That was Tuesday afternoon.

The next day, Wednesday, the day of the Connollys' funeral, was unreal—because it was so ordinary. After what happened, knowing it was all so final, Cathy found it weird to see people carrying on in the same way over their same irritations. When she came down to breakfast, her mother was frying bacon. Her Mom glanced at the clock.

"Now, you just watch," she said. "Your father will walk in here in exactly two minutes. He'll open the paper and stand right there." She pointed to a spot in the middle of the kitchen. "Right where I can't get by without bumping into him. You wait and see."

At exactly seven-thirty, her father strolled in, took his usual stance in the middle of the kitchen, cracked open the paper to the sports section, and announced, "Giants have some good young players this season."

"Ralph," her mother said, "would you sit down, or go some place else to read the paper. I can't—"

Her father just stepped to one side.

"It would be different if we had a larger kitchen," her mother remarked, under her breath.

"That would cost a lot of money," her father commented.

"This kitchen couldn't be remodeled, for love or money," her mother snapped.

"I think it could." Her father seemed thoughtful, even a bit sad.

Her mother came from a prominent family back in Virginia, and when she married the bright young Stanford man, maybe she'd thought he'd end up being president of General Motors—or something. But, after a brief fling in private industry, her father had been swallowed up—her mother's expression, "swallowed up"—by the academic world. Cathy's mother, almost in revenge, slowly retreated into her world of television, movies, and the garden club.

"If your father sees the green of a dollar bill, he considers it vulgar, and runs in the other direction," she once said.

Like most sarcastic remarks, it contained a grain of truth. Cathy's father cared so little about money, he seemed almost disdainful of it. Except on occasions. Like this morning. Then he felt uncomfortable, a little guilty. Cathy could tell.

But he continued to stand in the middle of the kitchen, his juice in one hand, the paper in the other.

Cathy thought she just might scream.

What if she did? What would happen if she yelled it out loud? "Listen, Mom and Dad. There's a funeral today. A funeral for two people I killed."

Crazy thought. But what if she did? What would they say? What would they do? Tomorrow morning, would Mom still insist on a good hot breakfast?

Would Dad still stand in the middle of the kitchen reading the paper?

The rest of the day was equally fantastic. After school, at the Malt Shop, Deedee was complaining because her sister had cut Deedee's bangs too short.

"I could have killed her!" Deedee shouted, over the amplified chant blaring from the jukebox. "Honestly, I almost didn't come to school today, I look so awful."

"You look fine," Paul said.

"You're just saying that."

"No, I mean it. I like your bangs short, Deedee. The way you wear 'em most of the time, I don't know how you keep from going blind."

The Malt Shop was bedlam, waitresses mopping up spilled cokes and blobs of chocolate ice cream from the plastic-topped tables. High-pitched voices babbling, "That history quiz was murder . . . she's trying to flunk me."

This is indecent, Cathy thought. The four of us huddled together in the booth like this, surrounded by all this hubbub. We shouldn't be here. Everything's upside down and smashed, so how can we all sit here doing and saying the same things. She clutched Todd's hand tighter. Deedee knows this is indecent, Cathy told herself. She's just covering up, trying to make it easier by talking about her hair.

Cathy closed her eyes, trying, for a moment, to blank out the racket. When she opened them she was surprised to find Paul staring at her. His brown eyes were heavy and troubled. There was a rigid set to his mouth.

He remembers, Cathy thought. Maybe at least Paul remembers it's the day of the funeral.

The rest of the week passed with unnerving calmness. Every Saturday morning Cathy and Deedee worked at the Car Wash. The Car Wash was the Pom Pom's money-making project for cheerleader uniforms. Paul's father allowed the girls to use one of his filling stations, including all his equipment, for their ninety-nine cent wash jobs. Mr. Gerow didn't even take a share of the profits, so naturally all the girls considered Mr. Gerow the greatest.

Todd had made plans for the four of them to drive to Dodge Ridge to ski on Sunday, but it rained again. That meant it was snowing in the mountains, so they called it off. Cathy was glad. Somehow she didn't feel like getting up at four in the morning and fighting the slopes all day. She and Todd went to a movie Sunday night. Cathy was aware she wasn't keeping up in the personality department, but Todd didn't seem to notice. His behavior suggested he was pretty uptight too.

Monday morning something happened which shattered the unnatural calm. Cathy knew it was bound to happen sooner or later. She'd actually been preparing herself for it. But, it still came as a shock.

Cathy saw Mary Ann Connolly.

It happened between classes. Cathy was hurrying

down the crowded hall when she heard a girl in front of her say, "Look. There's Mary Ann!"

Two girls rushed over to Mary Ann. Cathy clenched her books to her chest and stood transfixed, as though somebody had tied her shoe laces together.

Mary Ann was tiny and blonde, the pale, delicate type. Her features seemed neatly sculptured, like her clipped, naturally curly hair. Her mouth and chin looked vulnerable somehow, giving the impression that if she smiled, she might have dimples. But Mary Ann wasn't smiling.

Cathy thought she knew everyone in school, at least by sight. But she couldn't remember ever having seen Mary Ann Connolly before. She wondered why. Was it because Mary Ann was so thin and wispy that she was the type you could easily overlook?

Cathy was unable to overhear their conversation. But she watched Mary Ann nod, then turn her face away, as if she were going to cry. Cathy found her feet and hurried down the hall.

She'd seen enough.

Cathy ran into Mary Ann again the next day, and the day after that. All week long, no matter where she looked, she seemed to find herself face to face with Mary Ann Connolly. And Mary Ann always wore that same look on her face—cowed, like an animal after a beating. And she was always wearing that awful brown plaid skirt and tan sweater. Cathy began to wonder if Mary Ann owned any other clothes.

Cathy speculated a great deal about Mary Ann. Where she lived, for one thing. Their suburban town didn't have what the newspapers termed "poverty pockets"—but some parts of town were shabby. Peach Street, where Mary Ann's parents had lived, for instance, and the old houses down on State Street which had been made into apartments, where Mary Ann had moved in with her grandmother after the accident.

Cathy got out the newspaper clipping describing the accident, which she'd hidden under the blotter on her desk, found the address of Mrs. Connolly's apartment, took the car, and drove by one afternoon. It was an old Victorian house converted into apartments, surviving like a weed among the new, modern apartment buildings on the street. The whole scene left Cathy feeling depressed.

But the thing that bugged Cathy the most was Mary Ann's clothes. Mary Ann didn't have many, and those she had looked as though they'd been picked up at the end-of-the-season sale. She confided this to Deedee one afternoon.

Deedee just shook her head and replied, "You might *know* that would be the first thing you're notice about Mary Ann—being as clothes conscious as you are, Cathy-baby."

"Thanks a lot," Cathy said.

But it was true. Cathy had an obsession. No, worse—a psychosis. She was becoming psychotic about Mary Ann's clothes. Cathy knew it was only a game, but when you worried about details, you didn't have time to worry about the whole, big, over-all picture. So Cathy concentrated on being psychotic about Mary Ann's clothes.

When she first got the idea, she didn't know. It had probably been in the back of her mind since she first saw Mary Ann. But the following Friday night she began to go through her wardrobe. Her mother was watching TV and her father had already gone to bed. At first, she pretended she was just cleaning out her closet. She was getting pretty good at kidding herself. Before she finished, she had a pile of clothes laid out on the bed, and she knew she was going to send them to Mary Ann Connolly —anonymously. She and Mary Ann were nearly the same size, though Cathy was taller, a size larger, maybe. Still, they could be taken in. She checked through the garments carefully, discarding the green and black plaid jumper. Too many people might remember that. The things she decided upon were all pretty basic. A red skirt and matching cardigan, though she didn't include the pink blouse she always wore with it. That, too, might be recognized. The pale blue knit—that was ages old. A white pull-over —everybody had white pull-overs.

She waited until the late show on TV was over and her mother had gone to bed. Then she found a box in the basement, packed up the clothing, tore open some plain brown grocery sacks for wrapping, and addressed the label to Mary Ann at her grandmother's apartment. She carefully copied the State Street address, using her father's typewriter.

It was nearly two o'clock in the morning when she finished. But she wasn't tired at all. She shoved the box under the bed, washed her hair, and climbed into bed. She felt better. It wasn't much, but at least it was something constructive to do. She'd mail the box in the morning, on the way to the Car Wash.

The worst parts of the days for Cathy were after school, at the Malt Shop. She found she dreaded that time more and more each day. But Todd insisted. To keep up the Couple of the Year image, she supposed. But to Cathy, at least, it began to be a drag, having to make like she was superhappy all the time. She began to count the days until the school election. Fourteen. Then spring vacation, when she had to go to the hospital to have four wisdom teeth removed. Even facing *that*, she wished the two weeks were over.

The following Monday afternoon Paul didn't show at the Malt Shop. Deedee slid into the booth, looking beat.

"Where's Paul?" Todd asked right away.

"He's not coming. He had to help his father at the filling station."

Todd frowned. "Well, he ought to show. The four of us always meet here after school. He knows that."

"It's not the 'Foursome of the Year,' you know," Deedee said, an evil glint in her eye.

"Look," Todd explained patiently, as if Cathy and Deedee were a couple of not too bright children. "Paul's one of us. He's part of our—"

"—happy little image?" Cathy could not help finishing the sentence.

Shocked silence. Todd and Deedee stared at her, unbelievingly.

Cathy's cheeks tingled. "I'm sorry."

Todd exploded. "What's eating you?"

She took a swallow of coke, but it didn't want to go down. "I'm sorry," she mumbled again. She wasn't sorry. With a shock she realized that this was the first time she'd said something to Todd that was unplanned, honest, with no thought as to how it would sound. It had just slipped out.

Deedee fished a crumpled pack of cigarettes out of her purse, and changed the subject. "Paul's going to join the Navy after graduation."

"Yeah, he told me," Todd said. "If it weren't for his lousy brother, Jacques, the Gerows could afford to send Paul to college."

"They can afford it," Deedee said. "Paul just wants to go in the Navy first."

"How come?"

"Who knows? Maybe he's reacting to Jacques."

"By going in the Navy? My God, that's not reacting, that's overreacting," Todd remarked cynically.

Jacques—leader of draft card burning,' one of the hard core in various college riots, though no longer a student—was twenty-three, married, and had a baby. Paul's father had been supporting his grandchild and daughter-in-law, ever since Jacques's unemployment insurance ran out. It was either that or let Jacques go on welfare, and Mr. Gerow was too proud for that. He himself had never gone to college—Jacques graduated from Berkeley—but had started working in a filling station. He now owned four. Mr. Gerow had worked hard all his life for his family, and now he was supporting his son's family. But, as everyone said, what else could the Gerows do? They couldn't let their grandchild go hungry.

"It's a damn shame," Deedee said. "Paul's got a 3.4 average. He could get into the University just like that!" She took a long drag on her cigarette and looked across the room.

Todd grimaced. "You shouldn't smoke so much, Deedee."

"My only vice! And the way you worry over it, Todd—it gets me right here." Deedee thumped her chest.

Todd's eyes narrowed. "What's the matter, you and Paul have a fight?"

"No."

"Then, what are you so uptight about?"

"Hey, you two knock it off!" Cathy interrupted.

"Boy, you'd think—" Todd began. Then he stopped, and shook his head. "What's the matter with you chicks anyway?"

Deedee continued smoking, working on looking

52

bored. Cathy tried to sip her coke. Things had changed, all right. The bond that held them together was beginning to strangle. All this bickering —it was easier when there was someone else around.

"Hey," Cathy said. "There's Jerry Miller. Let's ask him to join us."

She tried. At that point they were all trying.

CHAPTER 5

There had been a part in *Murder at Midnight* about how the murderer always returns to the scene of the crime. The next morning Cathy realized that sending the clothes to Mary Ann had been her way —subconsciously, at least—of returning to the scene of the crime. As in the play, she almost got caught.

It happened after study hall. The bell rang and Cathy was gathering up her books when behind her she heard a voice.

"Cathy?"

Cathy whirled around and found herself face to face with Mary Ann Connolly. Mary Ann was wearing Cathy's red outfit with a pink blouse! Cathy drew a deep breath and stood, motionless, unable to exhale.

Mary Ann smiled. "I just wanted to thank you for the clothes."

Cathy decided to fake it; the decision seemed to be no creation of her own, rather an instinct from outer space which flashed the message to her brain.

Cathy exhaled. "What clothes?"

Mary Ann touched the red skirt. "These. You did send them, didn't you?"

Cathy tried to keep a blank expression on her face, as though she might have been looking at anyone or anything, a chair, a door, a car. But all the while shock waves were exploding inside her head. Aside from the shock of Mary Ann knowing her name, knowing she'd sent the clothes, there was the final, additional shock of hearing Mary Ann's voice. Mary Ann Connolly's voice was light, soft—much like Cathy's.

"You did send them, didn't you?" Mary Ann repeated softly.

"I don't know what you mean." Cathy tried for a casual laugh, but it came out more like a yelp.

Mary Ann blushed. "O.K., if that's the way you want it."

Mary Ann might have dropped the whole subject then and there if Cathy had had enough sense to keep her mouth shut. But suddenly Cathy couldn't seem to stop talking. "I used to have a skirt like that—"

"I know." Mary Ann resumed the conversation quickly. "I remembered it. And the way you always wore the pink and red together. It was fantastic. So I put a pink blouse with it too." Mary Ann beamed. "You have a real feeling for colors. I guess that's why I've always admired your outfits."

Cathy could find no answer, except more lies. And it was obvious to them both that she was lying. This is really the bitter end, Cathy thought. She struggled to wake up from the feeling that must surely be a nightmare. She considered, briefly, fleeing—simply turning on her heel and running.

Then, without realizing it, Mary Ann saved the day. She said, "A lot of people have done nice things for me since the accident. Complete strangers. People I didn't know realized I existed."

Cathy swallowed hard.

Mary Ann spoke in a faraway voice. "It makes you feel good, you know?"

"Sure."

Mary Ann looked at the floor. "Well, thanks anyway," she said, and walked away without raising her head.

Deedee, of course, spied the red and pink outfit immediately and was waiting right outside the door after English class.

"You must have flipped! You must have completely flipped out of your mind!" Deedee shook her head incredulously.

"But Mary Ann doesn't suspect a thing," Cathy tried to explain, as they walked down the hall. "She said all sorts of complete strangers have done nice things for her . . ."

Deedee stopped in her tracks. "My God! You talked to her?"

"Mary Ann recognized the clothes, and thanked me."

Deedee closed her eyes, as though she were striving not to see the words she was hearing. "How could you give her your clothes? Just answer me that."

"I didn't give them to her. I mailed them to her. With no name."

Deedee blinked. "And she recognized them!"

"But she doesn't suspect a thing," Cathy explained again. "I just thought it would be something nice to do. I kept seeing her in that same skirt and sweater—"

"But you kept looking for her. You've got this guilt hang-up. You keep fooling around with Mary Ann Connolly and she's going to find out the truth. That's exactly what's going to happen."

"Deedee, don't tell Todd, huh?"

"Me, tell Todd? You think I want to break up the Couple of the Year? You must think I'm some kind of nut."

Deedee wasn't any kind of nut.

Cathy studied Deedee's white blouse, noted the perfection of each tiny ruffle, fluted like petals of a daisy, and wondered again how Deedee's mother could stand at the ironing board, guzzling booze and ironing such masterpieces at the same time. Mrs. Wyman must iron during the morning—her

58

"sherry hours"—not in the afternoon when she switched to something stronger.

People in town speculated; was it because of the drinking, or in spite of it, that Mrs. Wyman created the starched, wrinkle-free clothes that made Deedee look as though every outfit were brand new? But they never speculated in front of Deedee, because there was a wall around Deedee. When complimented, Deedee only replied, "My mother loves to iron."

Poor Deedee. No, Deedee wasn't poor; she was strong and beautiful and filled with conviction. Deedee never drank or smoked grass because, as she said, she wanted to stay on top of things. Deedee was anything but a nut.

"I promise. I won't have another thing to do with Mary Ann Connolly," Cathy assured Deedee.

Cathy meant it. Sincerely. She knew this would be the end.

After that, she tried to make sure Mary Ann didn't have another thing to do with her. It turned into a grizzly sort of game. When she ran into Mary Ann in the hall, Cathy would bend down and pretend to fix the heel of her loafer. When the bell rang after study hall, Cathy carefully engaged herself in conversation with the nearest person until Mary Ann had left the room.

The weather reports were good for skiing on Saturday. Friday night, as Cathy was getting her ski clothes together, her mother came to her room to talk.

The category for their nice little talk was: Todd Dillon.

"Honey, has anything happened between you and Todd?" Her mother made an effort to sound offhand, but to Cathy it sounded well rehearsed.

"No, Mom. Why?"

"I don't know. You've been acting funny lately."

"Funny—ha ha? Or funny—strange?" Cathy said, sticking an extra pair of socks in her ski boots.

Her mother ignored Cathy's attempt at humor. "Todd doesn't come over as often as he used to, and when he does, you . . . you don't sparkle."

"I don't?" Cathy asked, genuinely surprised.

Her mother was obviously finding this an unsatisfactory conversation. But she plunged on. "I think Todd's a fine boy with a fine future."

"Todd *is* a fine boy, Mom. He's going to a prep school in the East before he takes the entrance exams for West Point. Colonel Dillon doesn't want him to take the exams fresh out of high school. He doesn't think Todd's quite ready."

"Todd will make a good Army officer. Your cousin Winston went to West Point, you know."

"I know," Cathy answered, wondering what her cousin Winston had to do with Todd.

"A girl could do a lot worse than Todd Dillon," her mother said.

Cathy laughed. "What is it you always said, Mom? If a girl in Virginia is still unmarried by her

60

eighteenth birthday, she's considered an old maid?"

Her mother brushed this aside. "That was just a saying. I want you to go to college, of course. You shouldn't dream of marriage for years."

Cathy had never dreamed about what it would be like to be married to Todd; just being in love was happiness, going steady, the ultimate. She tried to visualize herself as Mrs. Todd Dillon—paying a formal call on the commanding officer, leaving their card in a silver tray, attending receptions, having garden parties with little watercress sandwiches. She'd probably have to roll her hair up *every day*. When Todd came home at night, she'd serve a gourmet dinner in white lace hostess pajamas. Candles, maybe?

Or would they go for an ice cream, then the movies, then bowling? Skiing every weekend, for sure. Pictures flashed through her mind, like those of a movie camera speeded up.

When would she have time to wash her hair, she wondered? Or read a Rod McKuen poem, or lie in the sun and daydream that she was somebody else?

Her mother was saying, "I don't want to interfere. You know that, honey. But has anything happened between you and Todd?"

Just the whole world, Cathy thought.

"No, nothing's happened," she said.

"You're so quiet and withdrawn these days. Even around Todd. Your father and I have noticed. why, when Todd calls, you meander to the phone like an old lady. You used to run like a chipmunk.'

"Mom, everything's fine. Honest."

Her mother stood up. "Well, if you're leaving at four in the morning, I guess you'd better get to bed early."

"I guess so. Don't bother to get up, Mom. We'll stop for coffee on the way and eat breakfast at Dodge."

Boy, she's sure switched, Cathy thought, after her mother left the room. When the boy she'd been going with moved to New York and Cathy had been stranded, she'd had casual dates with different boys.

Her mother, not understanding, had tried to cheer her up. "When I was a girl, I used to date lots of boys. The more boys you dated, the more popular you were considered. And you go with lots of different boys, dear. You really do."

She really did. That's what was so embarrassing.

Until that night at Deedee's house when she met Todd. From then on, everything was roses—for both her mother and for Cathy.

The skiing the next day was great—corn snow, but no sign of slush. The sun was blinding bright. They arrived at Dodge Ridge early. She and Deedee had a big breakfast. Todd and Paul had an outrageous breakfast—hot cakes, bacon, sausage, eggs. While the four of them ate, they watched the busses roll in. Every church group, every "Y" group, even a bunch of kids from Arlington High had chartered a bus that morning. The snowfall had been heavy during the winter, and people were predicting skiing until the end of May. But you'd think it was the last skiing of the season by the looks of things.

Todd and Paul, being experts, took off on their own. Deedee and Cathy made no effort to keep up. By mid-morning the slopes became more and more crowded, the lift lines longer and longer. By noon, the slopes resembled giant ant hills.

Cathy, practicing her stem Christies, was pleased with her progress. But soon there were so many skiers, she had several near collisions, and she was getting tired—the formula for a broken leg. She searched for Deedee, found her standing in line for the chair lift.

"Hey, Deedee, let's go eat, huh?" Cathy called.

"Now that's a real concept." Deedee dug her poles in the snow and coasted over. She took off her sunglasses and rubbed her eyes. "This is too much of a mob scene! Where are the boys?"

Cathy glanced around. "Who knows?"

"Who cares? Let's eat," Deedee said.

A voice boomed over the loud-speaker, warning of ski thieves in the area, so they each invested twenty-five cents to lock up their skis before leaving. They clumped up the long flight of stairs to the cafeteria. Inside, the place smelled of damp clothing and hot food from the steam tables. Snow had melted into little puddles of water on the floor.

"I hate spring skiing like this. Everything's soaking wet," Deedee said.

"It's better than blizzards, though. Remember

that time after Christmas when your hair turned to icicles?"

Deedee giggled. "And you wore the white face mask and Todd kept calling you the abominable snowman."

They were nearly through the cafeteria line when Deedee whispered, "Don't look now, but guess who's behind us?"

Cathy turned. "Who?"

"Don't look, I said." Deedee groaned. "It's her, all right. I'm sure."

"Her" had to be Mary Ann Connolly. Cathy could tell by the alarm in Deedee's voice.

A familiar sense of panic came over Cathy. "Well, let's find a quiet corner—"

"You're a dreamer. There's not a quiet inch in this whole place."

They finally wiggled into two places at one of the long benches on the sun deck. Cathy had a premonition that Mary Ann would appear in the doorway any minute. It happened, almost as though her thoughts had projected it into existence. Mary Ann stood on the deck with her tray, searching for a vacant spot just as a place opened up at their table.

"Perfect timing," Deedee said in a muffled voice as Mary Ann approached.

"Hi," Deedee said.

"Hi!" Mary Ann was delighted. "Mind if I join you?"

Cathy smiled. "No, sit down."

Mary Ann sat across from them. What difference does it make if Mary Ann's wearing wool slacks instead of real ski pants, Cathy asked herself. Why do I notice things like that?

"Did you come up on the bus from school?" Deedee asked.

"Yes." Mary Ann's eyes were shining. "It's the first time I've ever skied too. I was so scared. Liz McKneally, the girl I came with, is an expert. I've lost her. She's probably on top of some mountain."

"The fellows we came with are too good for us. We've lost them too," Cathy said.

"Did you take a lesson?" Deedee asked politely.

"Did I ever!" Mary Ann beamed. "I learned the snow plow. I mean, I was supposed to learn the snow plow. Actually, I learned the correct way to fall down. Could you believe that's the first thing the instructor taught us? I thought he was fooling, but now I think knowing how to fall is the most important thing of all."

Deedee gulped her chili, doubled over, and began to cough. And cough. And cough.

"Hey, Deedee. You all right?" Cathy slapped her between the shoulder blades. But Deedee kept on coughing. "Deedee?" Cathy leaned over, genuinely concerned.

When her face got close, Deedee whispered in a strangled voice, "Here come the boys!"

Cathy jerked around and stared over the railing. Todd and Paul, skis balanced on their shoulders, were walking across the parking lot to the cafeteria.

"Excuse me." Deedee stood up. "Something must have gone down the wrong way."

"Here, have some water," Mary Ann offered.

"No. No, thanks. You kids finish. I'll just—" They never heard the rest of the sentence because Deedee, no longer doubled over, was pushing and shoving her way across the crowded deck.

Deedee, please think of something. Todd will flip if he finds me here with Mary Ann. I can't get up and leave. Or can I?

"Maybe I'd better go see if she's all right," Cathy said tentatively.

"She'll be O.K.," Mary Ann replied innocently.

Cathy tried to hurry. The chili was so hot, both with fire and seasoning, that her throat closed tighter with each swallow.

Deedee will stall the boys. You can depend on Deedee. It was a prayer.

Cathy tried to think of something by way of conversation. "When you've practiced enough, you can get off the rope tow. Then it's a lot more fun. I hate rope tows. They wear you out." Cathy realized she was rambling. But she couldn't just sit there.

"It's my skis. The tips keep crossing," Mary Ann explained.

"How long are your skis?"

"I don't know. I borrowed them from Liz McKneally's brother."

"Oh. Then they are too long. It's easier, the shorter they are."

"Do you have your own skis?" Mary Ann asked.

"Yes, I got them a year ago Christmas."

"That must be great," Mary Ann said admiringly.

"Well, unless you ski a lot, it's cheaper to rent them."

"I suppose so. It took all my baby-sitting money just for the bus ticket and the ski lesson."

"Oh," Cathy said. "Well, it's an expensive sport."

"Gosh, Cathy, aren't you excited about being nominated for Couple of the Year?"

Cathy was flustered. "I don't know. It's just a contest."

"I bet you're going to win though. All my friends are going to vote for you."

Cathy gawked. "They are?"

The people next to them got up and left. For the moment she and Mary Ann were alone at their end of the bench. There was an awkward pause.

"Gosh, Mary Ann"—Cathy found it hard to say her name out loud; they'd always referred to Mary Ann as "she" or "her"—"you don't have to ask your friends to vote for me. For us, I mean. If it's because of those clothes, forget it. You didn't tell anyone, did you?"

"No. Not that I didn't want to." Mary Ann propped her elbows on the table and leaned forward. "You know, with your father being Dean, and you going steady with Todd Dillon, being a Pom Pom girl, all those things . . . well, sometimes people are just plain jealous of someone like you. Because you have everything. What people don't realize is, you *have* everything because of the kind of person you are underneath. But kids don't stop to figure that out. All they see is that you're popular, one of the top girls at Arlington."

"But I'm not! That's just it!" Cathy gave up trying to eat and pushed the bowl aside.

But Mary Ann didn't seem to notice, because she kept on speaking in the same confidential tone. "It's things like you caring enough for somebody you don't even know . . . to do nice things for that person . . . and not even expect to get credit. That's the kind of stuff people don't know."

Cathy wanted the earth to open and swallow her up.

Mary Ann flushed. "I'm sorry, I didn't mean to get sticky. Maybe I *should* tell people how nice you were. But I'm afraid they'd think you were just trying to get votes. Some people are always ready to believe the worst, you know."

"The clothes were nothing. Honest. And I don't want you to tell anyone."

"I haven't," Mary Ann assured her. "Besides, I guess I'm too proud. I don't want people thinking I accepted charity."

"It wasn't charity and you shouldn't mention it to anyone. I don't want you to," Cathy's voice rose to an alarming pitch.

"I won't. But I can get my friends to vote for you and Todd." Mary Ann had finished eating.

Cathy stood up. "There're people standing in line. We'd better go."

Mary Ann glanced at the bowl of chili. "You're not going to finish?"

"No, it's . . . horrible."

On the way downstairs Mary Ann turned to her. "I'm going to the little girls'. Want to come?"

"No," Cathy said. "I think the others are waiting. I'll see you later."

" 'Bye then." Mary Ann walked down the hall.

She was, Cathy decided, getting a bit tired of explanations.

"What took you so long?" Deedee was demanding.

"I told you. I got away as soon as I could."

They were waiting in line for the chair lift. When their turn came, Deedee and Cathy got in together. With a slight jerk, the chair started up.

"If you had any idea of the contortions I went through to keep the boys downstairs!"

"I know, Deedee. I know. I appreciate it. I really do. But it was just one of those things."

"It wasn't one of those things."

"What do you mean by that?"

"Those things just don't happen. You attract that girl like a magnet, or your guilt attracts her like a magnet, or something."

Cathy looked down at her skis, dangling in midair, then at the snow-covered pine trees, so close you could almost reach out and touch them. Everything seemed so white and peaceful, she wished she could get off the lift right now, lie in the untouched snow and gaze up at the dark green undersides of the pine boughs. She envisioned the snow as a white blotter that would soak up all the hurt; the giant pines would ask no questions, bestow no compliments, demand no explanations, tie no knots in your stomach. The trees, standing quiet and unperturbed, would bring peace.

When they were nearly to the top, Cathy gave it one last try. "Deedee, I promise I'm not going to have anything further to do with Mary Ann Connolly. And that's that."

Deedee brushed a strand of her hair from her face. "It's not that I care, Cath. It's Todd. He'd kill you if he knew."

CHAPTER 6

They stopped for hamburgers on the way home, and for a while it was almost like old times. Todd was in a good mood, Deedee apparently over her mad, and Paul, mimicking Deedee getting off the chair lift, gave them a lot of laughs.

The important thing was to keep from making waves, Cathy thought. And any contact with Mary Ann Connolly—no matter how casual—was making waves. Cathy fully intended to keep her promise about not having another thing to do with Mary Ann. What she hadn't planned on was Mary Ann having another thing to do with her.

Cathy received the news Monday morning in the main lobby, right inside the front door of school. There, leaning against an easel, stood an enormous black and white poster, done in charcoal, showing Cathy and Todd sitting on top of a windswept

Earth. Other, smaller planets, and shooting stars whizzing through space, formed the background. The caption read: "Cathy and Todd—Couple of the Universe." In the lower right-hand corner, "M.A. Connolly" was printed in small letters.

Cathy would have sworn that by now she was shock-proof. But the sight of the poster struck her like a physical blow.

Someone standing nearby said, "Boy, that's the coolest poster yet!"

"If you don't win with that!" another voice cried.

"Hey, Cath, I thought you and Todd were running for Couple of the Year, not the Universe."

Cathy, still reeling, managed to reply. "I guess she took artistic license—like poetic license."

A third voice spoke up. "Mary Ann's fantastic. You know, she's going to apply for a scholarship to art school when she graduates."

Cathy turned. Liz McKneally, Mary Ann's friend, was standing next to her.

"I hope she gets the scholarship," Cathy said politely.

Liz stood back, cocked her head to one side, and said, "You know, she ought to keep that poster for the Scholarship Committee."

"She sure has talent," Cathy commented.

"You'd better believe it." Liz continued to admire the poster.

The rest of the morning Cathy went through the motions of attending classes and accepting compliments on the poster, all the while hoping she wouldn't run into Mary Ann. She'd have to thank Mary Ann, of course. But first she had to face Todd, Deedee, and Paul at lunch. That would be a full-scale senate investigation. She had not the remotest idea of what she'd say or how she'd explain. She wasn't even supposed to *know* Mary Ann. Or vice versa. She needed time to think, time when her head didn't feel as though it were about to float off. Perhaps she should go home for lunch. She considered getting sick. That wouldn't be hard to do; she was close now. But all the while she knew she wouldn't come up with explanations tomorrow, or the next day, or next week. There was nothing left to do but get it over with today.

At lunch time, Todd, Deedee, and Paul were sitting at their usual table, waiting for her. Their three faces seemed carved in stone, like the faces at Mount Rushmore, she thought giddily.

The school cafeteria was always noisy with hundreds of voices trying to compete with the sounds of clanking silverware and hundreds of other, louder voices. Today the din was ear-splitting. Perhaps that was why, after she sat down at the table, she began to talk too loudly.

"Listen, kids, I won't be able to make the Malt Shop today because I have to go to the oral surgeon's for a 'preoperative' checkup. That's what they call it, 'preoperative.' The operation is Saturday morning at All Saints' hospital."

They didn't seem to be listening.

"Well, have any of you guys ever had four wisdom teeth cut out all at once?" she continued. "Two of them impacted! I mean, it's not going to be any picnic. I won't look so great by the time they're through. In fact, it's lucky the 'Couple' election is Friday, Todd. You wouldn't stand a chance to win on Saturday. Not with me for a partner! I know I'll have to come home from the Spring Formal early Friday night. Actually, I'll be lucky if Dr. Denny doesn't tell Mom I can't go to the formal at all!"

Deedee's face was ashen. "I told them, Cath— about the clothes."

"Oh."

"Well, for heaven's sake, I had to tell them. How else could I explain the poster?" Deedee said miserably.

The three of them watched, waiting for her to say something. Like a computer programmed to give the only possible answer, Cathy said, "I'm sorry about the clothes. I didn't mean to start anything."

"O.K.," Paul jumped in. "Let's not make a federal case out of it. Cathy sent the stuff. Mary Ann made the poster to say thanks. They're even now, so that ends it."

But it wasn't ending it for Todd. He glared at Cathy, as though examining some unexplanable new form of human.

In desperation Cathy tried to back up, start all over again. "No kidding, Todd. Having to have four wisdom teeth out Saturday, I may not be able to go at all on Friday . . ."

Todd continued to stare. When he finally spoke, his lips were so tight she could barely hear his words. "You keep messing around, and that girl's gonna find out the truth. You know that, don't you?"

Paul gave a long, tired sigh. "Aw, cool it, Todd."

"Cool it? That's a laugh. We all agreed to—the day after it happened." Todd turned on Paul. "Right in the parking lot, sitting in my car. Remember? Then little Miss Guilty here gets the bright idea—"

"I told you, I didn't mean to start anything," Cathy cried.

"We tried to protect you, but you're asking for it. This Mary Ann's gonna find out. And when the beans start spilling all over the place, there's gonna be a lot of people hurt!"

Cathy met Todd's eyes. "For instance?"

"For instance, me . . . you . . . all of us!"

"But you didn't make the phone call, Todd. I was the one. It's my little red wagon—" Cathy clenched her fists tight. "Todd, you mean . . . it's not about the Couple of the Year bit? It couldn't—"

But she could tell by his face, that's exactly what it was about. She spread her hands in a helpless gesture. "A silly little school contest? It'll be over day after tomorrow."

"O.K.," Todd said. "So maybe it's a silly little school contest. But being a part of a nasty story like this wouldn't help any of our reputations."

"Knock it off," Paul warned.

"No, let him go on." Cathy's mood changed to one of defiance. Because now she was remembering the night of the phone call, the big joke about going with the Dean's daughter so he could get a recommendation for West Point. Now she was getting a lot of answers. Fast.

Todd turned to Cathy and said, "Actually, I'm worried about you, Cath. Your guilt complexes, your do-good complexes! Christ, while you're at All Saints' Saturday, why don't you apply for a job as a volunteer? There're all sorts of down-and-out people you could be helping—"

That did it. She could stand anything but his sarcasm. Her defiance vanished, and though she loathed herself for it, tears rolled down her cheeks. The kids at the next table stopped eating and stared at her. There was a curious moment of embarrassment during which Todd, Deedee, and Paul all looked away.

Then Todd pushed back his chair and stormed out of the cafeteria.

Deedee followed him, trying to sooth troubled waters, Cathy supposed.

Slowly Paul's hand crept under the table; his fingers closed about her wrist. His touch was warm and reassuring, and when Cathy looked up, there was something resembling understanding in his eyes. Understanding? This had to be some kind of miracle, because who in this world could *understand?* Cathy didn't understand herself, or Todd, or anybody else.

The two of them sat there, holding onto each other, sharing a tiny island amid all the noise and clatter of the cafeteria, and Cathy had the craziest desire to put her head on Paul's shoulder and sob. The sight of Paul's face, warm and strong, made her feel like a wanderer in a storm who has just sighted a light, a house, and a hearth.

Paul had always been one of the foursome. Now it was different. Now a spark of empathy flickered between the two of them. Now it had changed into a twosome. Maybe the feeling was only on her part. But Cathy realized that whatever it was—and she couldn't have defined it for the world—the feeling was genuine. And everything else in the world was so phony.

Paul must have sensed something, because he dropped her hand and stood up, looking confused. But his voice was tender, and his words just for her. "You do what you think is right, kid."

Then the moment was gone.

But not the memory. She carried the memory with her like a locket, close to her heart. It was the one something she could hold on to.

She did not go to the Malt Shop after school. The others probably hadn't either. She didn't know. She didn't really care.

It was quite a day for surprises. When she got home, her mother was poised in the entrance hall, fanning herself with a thick, white envelope.

"Open it, honey. It's from the college. It's your acceptance—or, but they wouldn't *dare!*"

Her mother extended a shaking hand, and Cathy took the envelope. Her mother moved closer, looking over her shoulder. "It was all I could do to keep from opening it!"

Cathy inserted her finger under the flap, and withdrew a sheath of paper. One of the sheets dropped to the floor. They stared at it. It was a printed form, "Application for Dormitory Space." That's when they knew she'd been accepted by the "good girls' school" in Virginia. Later, when they pulled themselves together and had spread all the papers on the coffee table in the living room, they found the nice formal letter of acceptance.

Her mother threw her arms around her. "I'm so happy for you, honey. I'm so happy. Wait until your father hears. Where is he? Still at school, probably. Why don't you call him?" Her mother stood back, and sighed, regarding Cathy as though she were seeing a preview of coming attractions at the movies. "Just as I'd always planned, a good girls' college in Virginia!"

"Right next to a good boys' college. Remember?" Cathy laughed.

"And if Todd gets into West Point—it's not that far away—he might ask you up for June Week!"

"Oh, he'll meet someone else by that time," Cathy said.

"Why, honey, what do you mean, 'someone else'?"

What Cathy meant was, Todd would no longer need Dean Shorer's daughter if he got into West Point. In fact, Dean Shorer's daughter was right now turning into a liability. But she couldn't spoil her mother's happiness, not this afternoon.

"Todd would love to have you up for a hop. The hops at West Point are so elegant," her mother said dreamily. "Everything's done . . . just right, you know. At least it was in my day," she added.

"Sure, Mom."

When her father arrived, he was equally enthusiastic.

"Now you won't be known as Dean Shorer's daughter," he announced with a wry smile.

She wondered how much difference *not* being Dean Shorer's daughter would make. Now that college in Virginia was a reality, some of the old self-doubt trickled back. She would be on her own, people would like or dislike her for herself. Would that mean starting all over again, in the looks department, the clothes department, the personality department? No, she could be her own self in Virginia. She wouldn't have to be anything big or great. No one would know anything about her. No one would know about Mary Ann Connolly, either. Except Cathy herself. Her whole future included the knowledge of what she'd done to an entire family, but no one in Virginia would know that. She'd never have to meet anyone's eyes who *knew*. What would it feel like? Freedom? No, never really. But maybe, just possibly, time would blur the image of Mary Ann Connolly.

At the thought of Mary Ann, Cathy realized that in all the confusion, she'd never even thanked Mary Ann for the poster.

"Hey, I almost forgot. I've got to make a phone call," she said.

Her mother beamed. "Now, which one are you going to call first? Todd or Deedee?"

I'd like to call Paul, Cathy thought. But she said, "I have to call this girl first. She made a poster for Todd and me—"

"I saw the poster." Her father was lighting his pipe. "The little Connolly girl, the one who lost her parents in the car accident made it, didn't she? It was good. Quite a compliment to you. I didn't know you knew the Connolly girl, Cathy."

"I don't. Well, just slightly."

"It was quite a bit of work for someone who knows you only slightly," her father remarked.

She had to be careful. The structure of her life was composed of lies built on top of lies, and one casual slip could bring the whole thing down.

"I'll phone the Connolly girl first. Then I'll call the other kids," Cathy said carefully.

Her father put down his pipe and regarded Cathy thoughtfully. She'd always cherished the closeness between herself and her father. Now she realized the very thing she'd cherished could turn into danger.

She opened the phone book to look up Mrs.

Connolly's number. It gave her an odd sensation, having to look up that number.

That night, as her mother was taking up the hem in her formal, Cathy said, "If Dr. Denny's going to operate so early Saturday, maybe I shouldn't go Friday night."

Her mother's face registered shock. "And miss the Spring Formal?"

"It's not such a big deal."

"With you and Todd up for Couple of the Year?" She was dismayed. "You have to have Todd bring you home early, of course."

"O.K. I just thought—"

"Thought what, dear?" Her mother was genuinely puzzled.

"Nothing. Forget it," Cathy said.

Cathy was thinking that her mother ought to forbid her to go to the Spring Formal, like she had when Cathy was little and she used to forbid her to go swimming for one whole hour after eating. Cathy wanted the kind of big, final, irrevocable "No" now. But she was only getting "Yes."

Friday took a hundred years to come, but it finally arrived—bright and sunshiny. The atmosphere in school was electric with excitement.

That afternoon she and Todd won Couple of the Year.

The voting took place in the gym, and while the ballots were being counted, everyone stood around in a state of tension. The editor of the school paper climbed on top of a chair to announce the winners, and when he pronounced Cathy's and Todd's names, big cheers went up and all their supporters seemed real jazzed.

Todd put his arm around Cathy and gave her a big kiss in front of everybody. It passed through her mind that this *had* to be the phoniest part of all.

Then everybody was congratulating them, and everybody included Mary Ann Connolly. "I'm so happy for you," she squealed, her eyes sparkling with excitement.

"It was your poster that did it," Cathy said, feeling tears come to her eyes.

"Oh, that? That was nothing."

"Congratulations!" someone else said.

"Hey, you're crying," Todd laughed nervously.

"I can't help it . . . it's . . . it's so fabulous," Cathy lied.

In his quick, smooth manner, Todd led her out of the gym, his grip firm on her elbow.

Out of the corner of her eye, she saw Paul his hands shoved in his pockets, standing to one side. She thought if Paul would just come over and stand near her, it would help somehow.

CHAPTER 7

Well, Todd had his Couple of the Year, she thought as she dressed for the formal that night. That was something. At least somebody had something they wanted.

So she really shouldn't have been so surprised when he dumped her. She just didn't think it would be so soon, not the same night. It was like burying the body before it had a chance to get cold. And that was too much!

They left the formal early as planned. When they got to her house, Todd parked in front and turned off the lights as usual. But he didn't reach over, or put his arm around her. Which was O.K. with Cathy.

"I've applied for a job with the phone company for the summer," he said, turning down the radio.

"Good." She drew up the collar of her coat. "It's

cold. Want to come in a minute? I promised Dr. Denny I'd get eight hours sleep, but there's still time—"

But Todd wasn't listening. "And then . . . well, if I get the job, it'll be manual labor, putting in new poles. I suppose I'll be pretty pooped by the time the day's over. In fact, the job may not even be in the Bay Area. They sent some of the guys up to Oregon last summer."

"Exactly what are you trying to tell me, Todd?" She wasn't going to make things easy for him.

He turned up the radio. "It's just that once school's out, it looks as though I'm not going to be around as much."

She got the message. "You mean, this is like two weeks notice?"

"I don't get you—"

"Two weeks notice, four weeks notice? I'm being fired as the other half of the Couple of the Year. Right?"

That must have shaken him, because he didn't answer for a minute. Then he laughed. "Aw, come on, Cath."

She opened the car door. "Well, that about wraps it up, doesn't it?"

He put his hand on her arm. "We can still see each other until graduation."

"No thanks, Todd. Let's just call it quits."

"You're mad," he said.

"I'm not mad."

"Yes, you are. Listen, Cath, I want you to know

I think you were a good sport about the 'Couple' business. I know it didn't mean as much to you—"

She shrugged. "Think nothing of it. I try to spread laughter and cheer wherever I go."

"Don't, Cath. Please. You're so bitter."

Todd was right, of course. Maybe for a change she should try to look at things from his point of view. "It might have been different, Todd. Except everything got so fouled up after the phone call. *I* changed."

"You can say that again." He touched her shoulder. "You're a good kid, Cathy. Almost too good. I mean, that's your real hang-up. That's why things get so complicated for you."

She couldn't think of an answer.

He took his hand away and stared into the night. "Well, no matter how you slice it, I guess you'd have to say we're just not the same type any more."

"Know something, Todd? We never were."

Looking back, she decided the conversation in the car had been merely the formalities. They'd broken up long ago—the night of the phone call, to be exact. The whole exciting romance had gone —plunk. Now all that was left was a cheated, let-down feeling, like discovering the beautiful pearl in your ring had been made of paste all the time.

That night, getting ready for bed, her hands shook so, she could hardly unfasten the clasp on her watch. She got a glass of water, opened the little envelope, shook out the two yellow "nerve" pills she was supposed to take first thing in the morning. She didn't know how her nerves would be in the morning, but they couldn't be any worse than right now.

Maybe the pills knocked her cuckoo, because that night she had a dream—a nightmare. In her dream she was older, but Mary Ann was still a little girl. Cathy might even have been Mary Ann's mother, in the easy way relationships change in dreams. It was very cold and foggy and she was supposed to meet Mary Ann at the school bus so that Mary Ann wouldn't have to walk home. But she couldn't get the car started. So Cathy ran all the way to the bus stop, without even stopping to put on her coat, because she had the funniest feeling—a premonition, sort of—that Mary Ann was in some sort of danger.

When she got there, Mary Ann jumped off the bus with Liz McKneally. They were both laughing. Cathy turned away, thinking what a dope she'd been. Then she heard the screech of brakes, and whirled around. Mary Ann was standing in the path of an oncoming truck. Cathy, the mother, sort of flew through space, as you do in dreams, and grabbed Mary Ann out of the way the instant before the big, double tires would have flattened her onto the pavement.

Then Todd appeared out of nowhere. Cathy said, "See? I told you! I knew she was in trouble!"

But Todd only laughed. "Things get so complicated for you, Cath."

The dream ended there, or if there were more,

she could not recall it. She got up the next morning feeling rotten. The details of the dream were already turning shadowy, but the eerie, crazy, illogical compulsion to save Mary Ann while there was still time remained. What did it mean? If there were such things as premonitions or warnings, the dream came weeks too late.

Having four wisdom teeth removed turned out to be an almost total blank, because, with all the shots and pills, she turned into a happy hunk of protoplasm. Until later, when all the lovely medicines began to wear off. Her mother sat by the bed, looking relieved because it was all over. But for Cathy, troubles were just beginning. Her entire jaw was one throbbing hurt. Her mother stayed for a while, assured her she'd be able to come home the next morning, told the nurse to take good care, then departed.

The nurse gave Cathy a pill and an ice pack, and declared in a booming voice, "I don't want any trouble out of you, Chick. I've got a whole floor of sick people, and you're not one of them."

The nurse had just stepped into the hall when Cathy heard her say, "Only stay a minute, Mary Ann. She feels like hell. By the way, isn't your grandmother working in pediatrics now?"

A grenade of pain exploded inside Cathy's jaw. She was in no mood to increase her misery by seeing Mary Ann. Instinctively, she closed her eyes, pretending sleep.

Her mother always maintained that while California flowers were beautiful and all that, they didn't smell beautiful—in fact, they had no scent at all. Not like flowers in Virginia, she was fond of pointing out.

But her mother was wrong, because Cathy could smell roses; the heavy fragrance was overpowering. She lay still, listening to the sound of footsteps hesitating inside the door, then tiptoeing across the room and finally, thankfully, out again. The scent of roses lingered in the room like a blanket of perfume. Cathy lay with her eyes closed for several minutes.

Then the nurse sailed into the room. "Boy, *she* sure got the cold shoulder!"

Cathy opened her eyes. "Who?"

" 'Who?' you say. Mary Ann Connolly, that's who! She comes all the way up here to see you, brings flowers—and you play possum."

"I was asleep."

"Who are you kidding?"

Cathy felt an overwhelming desire to bawl. But she wouldn't, not in front of the nurse. "It hurts so bad, I can't stand it. Could I have another pill?"

"Your chart says one pill every four hours, and it's going to be every four hours. You want to turn into a junkie or something? I'll get you another ice pack. We're pushing ice packs today."

"Thanks."

The nurse's voice softened. "Don't worry, Chick. The worst is over. From here on, it's all downhill."

The nurse brought two ice packs. Cathy propped them against her cheeks and tried to get comfortable. After a while, the ice began to make the pain a little fuzzy, and she dozed.

She experienced a weird, detached feeling, as though she were observing her thoughts, instead of thinking them. She thought about her funny little English teacher, Mrs. Dana, and how the kids always laughed because of the way Ralph Waldo Emerson really turned her on. What were the lines Mrs. Dana was always quoting?

"Rings and jewels are not gifts, but apologies for gifts. The only true gift is a portion of thyself."

The clothes she'd so carefully packed up and sent to Mary Ann—they were, at best, an apology. If there were only some portion of herself she could give Mary Ann.

Cathy had a lot of time to think that day. By afternoon she was feeling better, at least for a few hours after each pill. So when Deedee arrived, shortly after a blessed white pill, Cathy was ready to talk.

"Deedee, know what I've been thinking?"

Deedee settled herself in the chair by the bed. "No, what?"

"I know you're going to think I've gone off my rocker, but here's the deal. I think you should put Mary Ann up for Pom Pom girl."

"Good God, you *are* on dope!"

"No. Listen, I've been thinking about this all day.

It's one thing we could do for her that would mean something. Actually, being a Pom Pom girl would give her . . . well, status. It would put her in the fun group."

"Cathy, you're out of your mind. 'Putting her in the fun group'—that's like offering a Band-Aid to someone who's bleeding to death. I mean, it just isn't that important after what's happened."

"But it's something. One little, unimportant something."

"What would Todd say? Have you thought of that?"

"Todd and I broke up last night." Was it just last night? It seemed a million light years ago.

"Oh, no!" Deedee leaped from the chair and stood, gaping down at Cathy.

"We just agreed we weren't the same type," Cathy said.

"You can't! Not after being Couple of the Year. You just *can't!* Oh, Cath, I'm sick. Honest. It's partly my fault. I was ugly to Todd—in fact, I've been bitchy to everybody lately. I don't know what happened."

"We've all been bitchy."

"What's happened to the four of us? Paul even! He's turned into the great stone face. He won't even discuss what happened that night. He gets mad if I even bring it up. He treats me like a child who doesn't understand the full implications . . . oh, everything!"

"Don't be sorry about Todd and me. In a way it's

a relief. The pressure's off. We don't have to pretend any more."

"But Todd's . . . I mean, most girls would give their eye teeth—"

"Don't mention teeth, please."

Deedee covered her face with her hands and laughed. "Cath, sometimes I just don't understand you."

"I don't understand me either. But this is something we could do—something positive."

"I mean, I don't understand about you and Todd," Deedee said.

"I'm not talking about Todd. I'm talking about Mary Ann Connolly and getting her into Pom Poms."

Deedee's eyes widened. "But that would mean you'd have to be around her. Doesn't that bug you?"

"Sure it does. But it would only be for a little while. We're graduating in June. We'll be gone next year. And if Mary Ann were in Pom Poms, it would be like . . . like we'd left her a legacy."

Deedee took out a cigarette. "Can I smoke?"

Cathy looked around. "I guess so. There's an ash tray."

Deedee made a big thing about lighting her cigarette. "I couldn't put her up," she pronounced finally.

"Why not?" Cathy asked.

"She wouldn't fit in, for one thing."

91

"What do you mean, she wouldn't fit? What's so great about Pom Poms?"

"She's not popular enough. She's not cute enough."

"We've got some creeps in Pom Poms, and you know it."

Deedee hung back. "If you're so hot to get her in, why don't *you* put her up?"

"It would be dangerous. You know that, Deedee. I took a chance when I sent her the clothes. After all, you're the one who knows her. You'd be the logical—"

Deedee was twisting the ring on her finger. "I'd just rather not, Cath."

"Why?"

She shrugged. "Maybe I don't want to back a loser."

"Deedee!"

"I know it's not nice to say, but in spite of everything that's happened, Mary Ann is a born loser. She always was. You've got to face it, my friend."

"You're a snob, Deedee."

"O.K., so I'm a snob."

They'd reached an impasse, and it was evident they both realized it. Deedee stood up. "I guess I'll be running along—"

"Deedee, please."

"We'd have to see her at the Car Wash every Saturday."

Cathy had thought of that. "It would only be for a month. Please." Cathy was begging now. "Just this one thing. For me. And I'll never ask you another favor, I promise."

Deedee marched to the bureau, dug a comb out of her purse, and began to jab at her bangs, which was a nervous tic Deedee had. Her face, in the mirror, was tight and remote.

Deedee was watching Cathy's reflection, too. Cathy supposed if they'd been actually facing each other, she would never have said what she did next. But the mirror gave Cathy a once-removed, second-hand feeling, as though the hospital bed might have been a psychiatrist's couch.

"Deedee, there's this thing I have when I first wake up in the morning. There're a few seconds when my mind's a blank. I've forgotten about the phone call and the accident, like it never happened. Then all of a sudden—bang! It all comes back." She paused. "And I keep wondering if there will ever be a morning when I won't have to go through the shock of remembering it all over again."

Deedee was still combing her hair, but she was no longer looking at Cathy. "You'll get over it," she said.

"When?"

"Someday. When the idea sinks in. I used to feel that way, too—when my parents got divorced, when I finally realized about my . . . my mother's drinking. You finally just learn to live with it."

"Then you don't think I'm going nuts?"

"You're not going nuts. You just know how to manipulate people."

"What?"

"Manipulate people—me, for instance." Deedee jammed the comb in her purse and snapped it shut. "O.K., so I'll put Mary Ann up for Pom Poms, if that'll make you happy. But she'll never get in. That's for sure."

The nurse barged in then and said it was time for supper and Deedee would have to leave.

"Feel better?" the nurse asked.

"You'll never know," Cathy sighed.

The Pom Poms held their regular meeting four days later. Cathy was still grounded because her face was swollen. She stayed home, giving Mary Ann's getting into Pom Poms lots of positive thought.

Deedee arrived at the house late that afternoon, good news written all over her face. "It was just an ordinary run-of-the-mill miracle, but Mary Ann Connolly is now officially a Pom Pom girl!"

"Deedee! You got her in!"

"I just proposed her. Several of the kids said they didn't know her, then Jodi said she felt sorry for her. But it was Dianne who pointed out we've gotten the reputation of pretty legs, and someone with a little talent would give Pom Poms some class. And everyone agreed that Mary Ann was real talent. So they took a vote and she got in!" Deedee paused for a breath. "So she'll be at the

Car Wash Saturday if she accepts, which she will, for heaven's sake. You'll be there, won't you?"

"Sure."

"You positive? Your face still looks like a blimp."

"I'm getting the stitches out tomorrow."

"Then you'll be all well?"

"I'm all well now," Cathy said.

"Good. One other item—Todd's been accepted by that fancy prep school for West Point in the East. That, with his father's connections ought to just about sew up an appointment to the Military Academy at some future date."

"Good, I'm glad," Cathy said. She found she really was. "I'm all set for Virginia, Paul's going in the Navy. You all set for Berkeley?"

Deedee nodded. "Now I'm getting recommendations for sororities. I hope I can pledge a good sorority."

"Knowing you, Deedee, you'll pledge the best."

"I don't know. The whole idea of Rush Week scares me."

"You? Scared? Don't be silly. You'll snow 'em."

Deedee jingled her car keys. "Well, I've got to run. See you Saturday."

Deedee started toward the door, then turned. "Oh, one last item. This is gossip, and you know how I abhor gossip."

"Sure, sure."

"Well, Todd's—he's been dating Allyson Troy this week."

"I couldn't care less," Cathy replied. Which was almost, but not quite, true.

Cathy had looked forward to this week of convalescence. She had wanted it to be a week with parentheses around it, when nothing happened—except getting Mary Ann into Pom Poms, of course. She wanted it to be a week when she could forget the past and not think about the future. She wanted a vacation.

There had been a few small waves, though. Like when they were getting into the car to come home from the hospital. Her mother asked where the roses came from. Cathy said Mary Ann had brought them.

"Oh, the little girl who made the poster. What did you say her name was?" her mother asked.

"Mary Ann Connolly. She's just one of the kids in school."

Her mother looked vaguely alarmed, like she always did when she couldn't place the name, or the family. Cathy wondered if it would make any difference if she said Mary Ann's family came from Virginia. (Which they might have, for all Cathy knew.) No, that would be wrong. Then her mother would try to place the Connollys of Virginia. It seemed incredible the way families in Virginia either knew, or knew of, all other families in Virginia. All other families that mattered, that is.

Her father suggested it was because cousins married cousins, so it was one big, happy family anyway. But her mother, who was both sensitive and proud of her Southern heritage, replied that *that* sort of nonsense had gone out with the Civil War.

Her mother stuck the roses on top of Cathy's make-up kit. They slipped to the floor and a few petals fell off. Cathy picked up the bouquet and held it carefully in her hands the rest of the way home.

Her mother said, "Well, you'd better call Mary Ann . . . Connolly, did you say her name is? Anyway, you should call and thank her."

Cathy wrote Mary Ann a note instead.

CHAPTER 8

Cathy couldn't understand her mother. One moment she was the oppressor, the next moment, the oppressed.

The same day Cathy returned from the hospital, her mother received the shocking news that the Crestwood Garden Club—her mother's one, big social Thing—had been divided into two separate groups, at the request of the ladies who lived in the big homes north of Sierra Way. The north-of-Sierra ladies decided that those living south of Sierra Way would be happier with their own separate garden club, which, after all, dealt with the problems of the smaller, less formal garden. They even came up with a cute little name for the ousted group, to which her mother had now been automatically assigned. The Woodcrest Garden Club! They hastened to add that, of course, they would all continue to be one big, happy neighborhood and would still get together on big community projects like the annual Christmas Decorating Contest.

"You've been jettisoned," her father said bluntly. "In this day of total integration, you've been segregated. Sierra Way is, figuratively speaking, like the old railroad tracks, upon which the south side is the wrong side to live."

"You always tie ideas in neat bundles, don't you, Ralph? And then give us the cold, dispassionate conclusions you so enjoy thinking up."

Her father regarded her mother with that bewildered expression he wore when he didn't quite understand what was bugging her. He tried to laugh off his blunder.

"Well, you ladies who live south of Sierra might get some placards and stage a demonstration."

But her mother was in no mood for jokes. Her mother, Cathy could tell, was close to tears.

Cathy sprang into the act. "Boy, that takes some nerve! First they dump everybody south of Sierra Way. Then to top it off, they even think up a name for the people they've dumped. Woodcrest! That's Crestwood spelled backwards. They ought to change their name to S.B.O.N.S.—that's 'Snobs' spelled backwards. If I were you, Mom, I'd tell them to—"

Her father was glaring at her, so she shut up. Neither of them seemed to be able to offer her mother any solace.

So, maybe it *was* a knick-knack little garden club.

Couple of the Year was a knick-knack little school contest. Pom Poms was a knick-knack group of high school cheerleaders. Everybody had their little knick-knack thing that spelled *status*. Status seekers! Weren't they all? Except her father, of course, who remained content in his ivory tower and came out only long enough to stick his foot in his mouth. "Get placards and stage a demonstration." Honestly!

It was painful to see her parents as people instead of loving hands, cutting a birthday cake, or stuffing a Christmas stocking with goodies.

Oh, God, it was painful just to exist.

She should ask Deedee sometime. Deedee had a Ph.D. in existing. Was there a secret to it?

On Thursday her father came home with the news that Todd had been accepted by the prep school.

"I know. Deedee told me yesterday," Cathy said.

"You've known since yesterday?" her mother asked. "Cathy, you march straight to the phone and call Todd and congratulate him."

That was the logical moment to break the news that she and Todd had broken up. But she was too chicken. She made some excuse about not calling right that moment.

Her mother had remarked several times that she thought it was strange Todd hadn't even come over to see her. Cathy just shuddered and said she didn't want anybody to see her in her present condition.

She knew she had to tell her parents about Todd sooner or later, but that was the big defect in her character—everything had to be later.

Later—Saturday morning—finally arrived. Cathy, applying extra coats of make-up to cover the faint bruises on her jaw, noted with satisfaction that at least the swelling was all gone.

Her mother called up the stairs. "I promised to set up tables for our last Crestwood Garden Club meeting, so I may not be home in time for 'Our Daily Life.' Would you be back by one-thirty to watch it for me?"

"Our Daily Life" was Mom's favorite soap opera on TV, and the plot was so involved, if she missed one episode it took her days to catch up.

"I'll be home," Cathy called down to her mother. "But I don't see why you've going to that stupid Crestwood—"

"Now, honey, we've been all over that," her mother said as Cathy came down the stairs.

"O.K., but sometimes I think I ought to charge you regular baby-sitting fees for watching your TV shows."

Her mother walked to the kitchen, opened the dishwasher, found a load of clean dishes, and pointed to Cathy.

"I thought I told you to empty this last night."

"Isn't Mrs. Young coming today?" Mrs. Young was the cleaning lady, who came on Saturdays.

Her mother frowned. "Mrs. Young has a million other things to cope with in this house."

That was a good word, "cope."

That's what Cathy had been doing all week, coping—watching Mom's TV shows, loading and unloading her spastic dishwasher, holding down the washing machine during the spin cycle to keep it from galloping out of the room.

But she stayed and unloaded the dishwasher, because she didn't want to get to the Car Wash too early. If she fiddled around home long enough, she'd arrive late, and most of the kids would already be there.

Most of the kids were there, standing around in the bright sunlight in front of the filling station. Everyone wore their worst grubbies; many of them were barefooted. Mary Ann stood to one side, absolutely rigid, wearing what had to be a brand new yellow shirt and matching pants. Poor kid, she'd gone out and bought a whole new outfit just for the occasion.

"Hi!" She brightened when she saw Cathy.

"Hi!" Cathy bypassed the group and made her way toward Mary Ann.

Mary Ann eyed the others nervously. "Gosh, I didn't wear the right thing, did I?"

"You look fine," Cathy said. "You'll get your clothes dirty, though. We always have water fights and stuff."

Mary Ann looked down at her perfectly creased pants. "That's O.K. They'll wash."

Cathy watched the others, clustered together in a group. Nobody seemed to be paying any attention to Mary Ann. Which bugged Cathy. So she took Mary Ann over and introduced her to a couple of girls. They said they were glad to have her join Pom Poms, with about as much feeling as though they were reciting their own zip code numbers. She shouldn't be angry, she told herself. Let's face it, the other girls didn't have a personal interest in Mary Ann Connolly. And she did.

Then Paul drove up in his wreck of a car, got out and strung up the banner between the gas pumps.

CAR WASH—NINETY-NINE CENTS
POM POM GIRLS—ARLINGTON HIGH

"O.K., gang, you're in business," he yelled.

"Excuse me," Cathy said to Mary Ann. She rushed over to Paul. "Where's Deedee?"

"She's not coming. Why?"

"Darn!" Cathy scuffed the side of the gas pump with her shoe. "I just wanted her here, that's all."

She turned around, staring at Mary Ann. Paul's gaze followed hers. Nobody could miss Mary Ann in those clothes.

"Oh." Paul blinked. Even a boy could see how out of place she looked, Cathy thought miserably.

"Paul, stick around, will you?" she said.

"Sure." Paul nodded.

Business was slow at first, so everyone gathered around the soft drink machine, gabbing. Cathy tried to include Mary Ann in the small talk, but Mary Ann hung back, self-conscious and quiet. Finally Jodi's parents drove in, then some teachers from the school, and after a while they were washing cars like crazy. Paul stayed, helping at the gas pumps, yelling playful insults at the girls from time to time.

"Gee, that new girl's really a worker," Cathy overheard Allyson Troy remark. Which was something, for Allyson to notice anybody! But it was true Mary Ann was knocking herself out cleaning the insides of the windshields and sweeping out the hard-to-get spots behind seats. Around eleven, Jerry Miller and a bunch of his friends drove in for gas. Jerry immediately began to give the Pom Poms a lot of gab about how *he* wouldn't let any broads wash *his* car.

Naturally, with that kind of an invitation, one of the girls squirted a hose all over Jerry's windshield. One thing led to another and pretty soon they had a big water fight going—the girls at the two hoses, and the boys retaliating with buckets of water. It was a real zoo, with Paul naturally joining in with the other boys, messing up his own father's place. Everyone was hopping around and yelling like Indians in a Western movie.

Then all of a sudden Cathy looked around and saw Mary Ann standing, all by herself, with a funny little smile on her face which was supposed to mean she was in on the fun. Only she wasn't.

The breath seemed to go out of her lungs. She searched for Paul. He was watching Mary Ann, too. Then he turned to Cathy, and for an instant their eyes met and said everything, with no need for words.

Then Paul did something Cathy would never forget. He grabbed a hose away from one of the girls and with a giant leap, and a war whoop, turned it on Mary Ann—full force.

The water splashed all over those new yellow pants, her hair streamed down her face and she ducked, shaking her head and coughing. When her head came up, she was laughing and her eyes were shining.

It was just about the most beautiful thing Cathy had ever seen. Paul's act seemed almost a ritual that brought Mary Ann into the gang, made her one of them. At least for the moment. Maybe for good. Who knew? Something caught in Cathy's throat. She turned away and thought, *Paul, I'll love you forever*.

Then Paul's father bellowed. "You kids knock it off. You're going to flood this place!"

With the chaos over, the girls went back to the soft drink machine and the boys drove off. But something had been established—a little bond of friendship, something to grow on. Mary Ann would be one of the Pom Poms yet.

Shortly after noon Cathy and Paul drove Mary Ann home. Mary Ann asked them in. She said her grandmother had baked a chocolate cake that morning and wouldn't they like a piece?

Cathy didn't want to. Chocolate was murder on her complexion, but she didn't want to anyway.

She didn't think Paul did either, but accepting Mary Ann's invitation seemed to come under the heading of unfinished business.

There was a sort of sadness about the old Victorian home on State Street—a feeling of decayed elegance. Parts of the gingerbread trim had fallen off, and nobody had bothered to put them back, which gave the house an undressed look. A row of neatly clipped hedges and large hydrangea bushes tried, but didn't quite cover the peeling paint around the front porch.

The rooms inside were big, with dark woodwork and high ceilings. But someone had managed to chop up the old home so that the rooms opened one after the other in a straight line, like cars on a train. The furniture was old and could have been shabby, except that everything was spotlessly clean.

So was Mary Ann's grandmother, Mrs. Connolly. White hair, white nurse's uniform, everything clean and neat, except her eyes, which were red from crying. Cathy noticed it the minute Mary Ann introduced them.

"I asked the kids in for cake, Mrs. Connolly," Mary Ann said tentatively.

"Fine." Her grandmother smiled a shaky welcome and dabbed at her eyes with the back of her hand. "Sit down. Sit down. Would you like milk, too? The coffee's still hot—"

"Milk would be fine for me." Paul twisted his neck as if his collar were choking him.

"How did the Car Wash go?" Mrs. Connolly asked.

"Great," Mary Ann said, closing the refrigerator door. "Except look at me. I'm a mess. We had a water fight."

Mrs. Connolly smiled. "So I see." But she said it in a nice way, like it's O.K., it must have been fun. Then she checked her watch. "I've got to run. I'm on at three, and I've got errands to do first."

Paul stood up, nearly knocking over the chair. "Glad to have met you, Mrs. Connolly."

"I'm glad to have met you, too. Come any time. Both you and Cathy."

She remembered her name. It gave Cathy an odd feeling.

After she left, nobody said anything, and it got embarrassing because just a minute before the room had been swimming with polite conversation.

Paul gulped his milk. "Your grandmother's . . . very nice."

Mary Ann's mouth smiled, but not her face. "Thank you." She traced her finger over the blue and white checked tablecloth. "She cries sometimes, since the accident. I guess you kids noticed—"

"I didn't notice," Cathy exclaimed nervously.

Paul shot her a look which said, *cool it.*

"Well, you can't blame her. It's rough," Paul said. Then, obviously searching for a change of subject, he blurted out, "She's a nurse, I see."

"Yes, she works the three to eleven shift at All Saints' now. She used to work the morning shift, but after I moved in, she changed. This way she's gone by the time I get home from school, and we don't get in each other's way . . ." Her voice dwindled.

Paul cut into his cake. "Is she . . . was she . . . she must have been your father's mother?"

"No. My real father died. After Mom married Mr. Connolly, he adopted me. So that's how I got his name. But I'm not really a Connolly, and she—" Mary Ann glanced toward the door—"she isn't really related to me. She's my stepgrandmother, actually."

"Oh," Paul commented.

"But she's been real good," Mary Ann added quickly. "Taking me in and all."

"Well, for heaven's sake," Cathy broke in. "Why shouldn't she?"

Mary Ann shrugged. "We never got along, exactly. When my mother and stepfather were living, that is. So under the circumstances . . ." Her voice trailed off again.

Paul looked uncomfortable. Cathy couldn't seem to swallow the piece of cake in her mouth. She remembered the story about Mary Ann running away the night of the accident, and how the police had to bring her home. So it was more than just a shock. She never had gotten along with her grandmother. Dear God, that wasn't fair.

Cathy struggled to think of something to say.

"She sure seems nice, Mary Ann."

"Mrs. Connolly? Oh, she is. The thing is, I was

such a brat to her. I was always doing things. I T.P.'d the front of her apartment building once. It was only two years ago and I suppose I was . . . well, I guess I had a poor attitude."

"Yeah," Paul smiled wryly. "That's what they always call it—'poor attitude.'" He shoved back his chair and stood up. "Hey, I've got a date with Deedee this afternoon. I can't spend all day with you two chicks."

Mary Ann apologized. "Gee, I didn't mean to give you the story of my life." She followed them to the door. "I hope you kids don't think I'm ungrateful, or anything like that. Actually Mrs. Connolly is a good Christian woman who's only doing her duty."

There was something about the way Mary Ann said "good Christian woman" that made it sound like swearing.

When they got in the car, Cathy counted to ten before she took a breath. "Did you notice how she called her grandmother, 'Mrs. Connolly?'"

Paul nodded.

Cathy wanted to cry and be done with it. But she couldn't. Not in front of Paul.

She wouldn't have either, if Paul hadn't started to yell. "Look," he hollered, "if she used to be a brat and T.P. her grandmother's apartment, that's one thing; so help me, that's not our fault. If living with the old lady isn't all peachy creamy, that's Mary Ann's problem."

"What do you mean, 'our' fault?"

"Cath, I stood right there and let you make that

phone call. I didn't make the slightest effort to stop you."

"It seems I remember you did."

It was his offering to take part of the blame that broke her up. She started to cry. "I promised my mother I'd be home by one-thirty."

"I promised Deedee I'd pick her up at one o'clock," he answered.

Then he swung his car into the Beach Road and they drove as fast as the old beaten-up car would take them, which wasn't very fast. Neither of them spoke. Paul parked the car, came around and opened the door for her. "Come on," he said.

They scrambled down the small rocky cliff to the beach. Paul, holding her hand, went first, leading the way. Though it had been sunny just a few miles away, the beach was cold, windswept and gray. The waves broke and crashed on the shore like silver suds. The sky was matted with clouds the color of gunsmoke, and a chill wind ripped at their hair and clothing. Paul picked up a flat stone and tried to skim it into the waves.

Cathy loved the beach when it was cold and raw like today. Nobody else was around on days like this. Paul could yell his head off, and it would only be a whisper beside the crashing surf. She could cry a hundred years, and it would only be a single drop in the dark, blue Pacific. She found comfort in being such a small part of the universe. It was a nice anonymous feeling.

"Hey, let's run," she shouted over the roar of the surf.

She ran first, but he caught up and passed her. They ran and ran, jumping over rocks, over long snakelike pieces of kelp, driftwood, giant logs, rusty old beer cans, charred wood from someone's beach fire. They ran, sometimes close to the shore where the white foam splashed against their legs, leaving them cold and tingling.

They ran until Cathy, all her energy spent, dropped to her knees and fell forward into the rough sand. After a moment she sat up, drew her legs close to her body and rested her chin on her knees.

Paul knelt down beside her.

"Cath?" He reached out, touching her arm.

"Did you ever just want to die?" she asked.

He sat beside her and drew her close. A moment later they were clinging to each other, two frightened specks on the shore of the whole Pacific Ocean.

He kept patting her shoulder awkwardly, and saying, "It's going to be all right, Cath. I promise it's going to be all right."

But she kept on crying and holding onto him as if he were the last human left on earth. She hoped he'd never let go.

He took out his handkerchief and dried her cheeks gently, as though she were a little child. "Hey, you got sand all mixed in with your tears. You're making mud pies."

She smiled.

Then he brushed her cheek with his lips.

She was surprised. Paul must have been, too, because he pulled back, scooped up a fistful of sand and let it dribble through his fingers. He was looking at her—not like she was a little girl, either.

Then he stood up, took both her hands in his, and drew her to her feet. "Cath? Cath?" His voice, so familiar yet so strange, kept repeating her name.

His arms went around her shoulders, his hands slowly moved down to the small of her back, and he drew her close to him. He kissed her—a long kiss—wild and fierce, like the pounding of the surf, yet tender and somehow familiar, as though they had kissed many times before, or perhaps were destined to kiss, right here on this very spot in the sand.

Suddenly he released her and turned away, facing into the wind, his shoulders hunched over. She ran to him. He looked down, his face urgent and questioning.

"Cath?" he asked once more, his voice low and fierce. He caught her hand, pulling her toward him.

Cathy broke away. "I . . . I've got sand in my shoes."

"Let's go," he said, turning toward the cliff.

Looking back, she guessed that Paul was even more shook up than she. As they got into the car he seemed stunned, his eyes glazed. He turned the key in the ignition, put the car in reverse and backed out, burning the tires.

"I'm sorry." He stared at the road ahead. "I didn't mean it."

"That's O.K."

They tore down the Beach Road, Paul's knuckles riveted to the steering wheel. Finally he said, "I guess we've just been through a lot together, kid."

"Sure. You can't go through what we've been through and not feel . . . something."

"Yeah. That's all it is," he said, like he wanted to believe it.

Cathy didn't believe it either.

114

CHAPTER 9

It seemed wrong, upon returning home, to find her mother in the living room poised like a tornado waiting to strike. It was wrong because she wanted to remember, while it was still fresh in her mind, the wonder of Paul's kiss, both wild and gentle at the same time; the feel of his arms; the ache in his voice asking, "Cath? Cath?" She wanted time to figure out why she got scared, what made her say she had sand in her shoes. And end it all.

But when she opened the front door and saw her mother, those magic moments on the beach were cancelled out, washed away like so many sand castles.

First her Mom was fired up because Cathy had missed watching "Our Daily Life." Cathy stood in the hall, absolutely numb with the irony of the whole thing. If missing a TV show was all her mother had to worry about, God bless her, she *was* lucky. Or was she? If her Mom had to live her life through other peoples' trumped-up troubles via the tube, if she didn't know (or had forgotten) the feeling of a kiss mixed with salt spray and sand, her mother was indeed, spectacularly unlucky.

When her mother finished with that category— the TV show came first; was it in order of importance?—she announced she'd heard some gossip about Todd and Cathy breaking up. Of course, she hadn't believed it for a moment, and had hotly denied the rumor to the ladies at the Garden Club. If Todd had dated Allyson Troy, it was simply because Cathy was laid up, recuperating from the wisdom teeth operation. Her words were spoken with conviction, but the expression on her mother's face was one big question mark.

Cathy had decided to endure her mother's wrath in silence and wait as patiently as possible for the end. But now there seemed no further point in evasion, so she told her mother it was true. She and Todd had broken up.

Her mother asked why Cathy hadn't told her, why she had to learn it at the Garden Club. Cathy said she'd meant to, but hadn't figured bad news would travel so fast. Her mother kept repeating one word, "why?" And the only answer Cathy could think of was Todd's reason why. "We just weren't the same type." This, of course, didn't satisfy her mother because she thought they *were* the same type. Cathy finally ventured the opinion that she and Todd had, in a way, really only used each other to win Couple of the Year. Now that the contest was over, they'd mutually agreed there was no need to go on.

Cathy hated talking in big generalities like this, because her mother wanted specifics. But one thing she knew for sure, she could never tell her mother about the whole mess. It would kill her. So she'd have to stick with half-truths.

Finally her mother calmed down. And, being a practical person, said, "Graduation's only three weeks away. Who are you going to Grad Night Dance with?"

Cathy hadn't thought about that. But now she did. She stood there a minute giving it her full attention. The only conclusion she could draw was that she didn't care. What was there left in the whole living world to care about?

"I'll think of someone," she mumbled at last, then escaped to the sanctuary of her bedroom. But it was too late. The memory of Paul's face and the touch of his hands pressing against the small of her back were already beginning to fade. She could only recall the ending, his words, "I'm sorry. I didn't mean it."

That was Saturday.

Sunday morning, after church, Deedee came over. She was all dressed up in a green silk print, white hat and gloves, looking very poised and lady-like. She was, too. Poised, ladylike, civilized—absolutely rational about the whole thing. If she'd screamed or gotten mad, it might have been different, Cathy realized later. Deedee followed Cathy upstairs to her room where they could, as Deedee put it, "talk." Cathy flopped on the bed. Deedee sat in the yellow chintz chair. But she didn't kick off her shoes or remove her gloves, so Cathy realized this was going to be important.

For openers, Deedee said, "Cath, we've been best friends for going on three years now, haven't we?"

Here it comes, Cathy thought. Dear God, how much does she know? She found she couldn't look Deedee in the eye. She couldn't look at anything except the stuffed panda on her bed.

"Paul was an hour late picking me up yesterday. He said he'd been with you."

"That's right."

"He told me all about going to Mary Ann's grandmother's and everything."

Cathy wondered how much "everything" included. "Well, we sort of got conned into going in for a piece of cake," she explained.

"That isn't what I've come to talk about, Cath."

"Oh?"

"No. I've come to talk about Paul. He seemed pretty upset, and when people get upset, they're liable to get mixed up . . . well, you know. I think girls have a kind of built-in radar about things like this, don't you?"

"Things like what?" Cathy managed stiffly.

"Just this. Paul's mine. And I'm asking you to leave him alone."

118

"Oh, Deedee!" Cathy looked up. "Honest . . . he doesn't . . . I don't . . . I *honestly* don't mean anything to Paul."

Deedee looked right through her. "Cath, I love Paul. I hope someday, after he gets out of the Navy, we can get married. I guess what I'm trying to say is this—haven't you hurt enough people as it is?" Then, without waiting, she added, "Would you hurt me too?"

Cathy's arms and legs were dead weights. Her body seemed one blob of sickness and confusion. The pitiful face of Mary Ann Connolly, and the nervous, good Christian grandmother flooded her vision. She remembered the pain on Paul's face, the disappointment in her mother's face. And now Deedee, formal and precise, asking that she too be spared.

She had always thought people wanted to be decent and happy, without getting in each other's way. But one person's hopes seemed to spill over, get tangled up with another's, so there was always the winner and always the loser. Or so it seemed. God help us all, winners and losers alike, Cathy thought.

That is when she gave up.

"Deedee, I swear, no matter what happens, I'll never hurt anybody again. Ever."

"Thank you." Deedee's voice trembled.

There was a long pause. "Anything else?" Cathy asked.

"Well, as a matter of fact, there is. Paul and I

discussed things yesterday . . . and we want you to know . . . I mean, we think it might help if you know we consider ourselves as much responsible for what happened. The guilt is ours too."

"That's very nice of you both," Cathy said politely.

"It's not just a gesture. We mean it," Deedee repeated.

Cathy flung the panda across the bed. It fell to the floor. "What difference does that make? Does it matter if it was 60 per cent my fault and 40 yours . . . or 90 per cent mine? I mean, if we could figure it out mathematically, would it change one single thing? Would it make any difference to those two people buried out there in the cemetery?"

Deedee made fists of her gloved hands and sat up straight. "Cath, why don't you climb down off the cross?"

For some reason that hit Cathy wrong. The deflated, loser feeling vanished, and she began to do a slow burn.

Her voice rose. "I'm getting a little sick and tired of everybody telling me what I should do, and what I should feel. I feel what I feel, *inside me*. And I do whatever it is inside tells me to do."

Deedee got a tight-lipped look, as if there were a lot of things she'd like to say, but wouldn't.

So Cathy barged on. "I've already told you I wouldn't have anything to do with Paul. Though, why you think he'd have anything to do with me is more than I can figure out! I won't hurt you or anybody."

"I knew we'd get back to Paul," Deedee snapped.

"Paul doesn't have anything to do with this."

Which wasn't true, because Paul had everything to do with it. Funny, Cathy thought, how people argue about one thing when the real reason they're arguing is about something altogether different.

"Well—" Deedee stood up. "I guess I'd better be going."

Cathy didn't answer. Deedee left and Cathy lay on the bed listening to the click, click of Deedee's little square heels going down the stairs.

Cathy reached down and punched the panda. That's about all she could do any more—punch stuffed animals. She couldn't get *at* anything because everything was shrouded in lies and make believe.

Make believe Paul doesn't mean a thing to you. Make believe that you wouldn't just die to have him hold you in his arms and love you. Make believe you're just wild, crazy about Mary Ann Connolly. Make believe that you're absolutely ape over her grandmother, and of course, you didn't notice she'd been crying. Make believe—everything!

There was one thing for real, though. What she'd promised Deedee about not hurting anybody. She wasn't going to. For the rest of her life! She'd wear the damn mantle of a saint if it killed her, but she'd never hurt another human being.

As if to prove her point, the following week, under her mother's supervision, Cathy addressed countless graduation invitations to her kin back in Virginia without one word of complaint.

With only three weeks till graduation the pace quickened. Finals loomed on the horizon, making everyone nervous. And on Saturday the Pom Poms held their annual June breakfast, this year at Allyson Troy's house. The breakfast turned out to be a luncheon and swim party.

"Boy, this will curdle the cream of society—when we show up!" Deedee flung her oversized white straw purse in the back seat of the car, then climbed in.

Cathy had picked up Mary Ann first, then swung by Deedee's house on the way to Allyson's.

Cathy surveyed Deedee in the rear-view mirror. "What do you mean, 'curdle'? Pom Poms *are* the cream of society. At least, at Arlington High."

Deedee was adjusting her headband. "So I guess Pom Poms are the best Allyson can do until something better comes along—like maybe the Junior League."

"What's the Junior League?" Mary Ann asked.

Deedee gave Mary Ann a sort of hopeless look, as if to say, if you don't know by now, dearie, there's no use explaining.

"The Junior League is the top layer off the cream," Cathy said, trying to make it a joke.

"Oh," Mary Ann replied.

It was difficult, when they were with Mary Ann, to keep from talking around her. In addition, there was always that creepy feeling you might accidentally slip and give something away. Today Deedee wasn't being much help. But Deedee's and Cathy's natural banter was strained these days. It had been, ever since the scene last Sunday in Cathy's bedroom.

Yet Cathy had kept her promise. All that week, whenever she saw Paul, Cathy behaved as though he rated a flat zero on her reaction meter.

"Well, anyway, it'll be fun to see the Troy mansion." Mary Ann settled back in the seat. "My grandmother saw it once on a house tour. She said it was fabulous."

"I was invited to Allyson's once. But I didn't go," Cathy piped up, then added, "That was when Todd and I were going together."

At the mention of Todd's name both Deedee and Mary Ann looked uncomfortable, as though she were speaking of someone recently deceased. "For heaven's sake, you kids don't have to look so grim," Cathy said. "Todd and I are—"

"Still good friends?" There was a note of hope in Deedee's voice.

"Sure," Cathy replied. "Even though he's going with Allyson now. Hey, don't you know he's out there using her pool all the time?"

Deedee leaned forward. "And the cabanas

around the pool? Have you heard about them? They've got six cabanas by the pool. You know, like private dressing rooms. But from what I've heard about Allyson's parties, it's not dressing that goes on in those cabanas!"

Cathy turned the car into the long curved driveway. They drove past masses of pink rhododendron bushes and suddenly they were in front of the enormous white stucco Spanish-type mansion. They parked in front, walked around back, up the steps to the terrace and the large kidney-shaped swimming pool. A red and white striped awning shaded the sliding glass doors of the rumpus room at one end of the pool. Some of the kids were already inside playing Ping-pong.

The six cabanas, with louvered doors, each painted a different color, flanked the other two sides of the pool.

"Ah, there're the cabanas," Deedee grinned with relish. "That's where the sinning goes on."

Mary Ann stared with wide eyes.

Allyson's party had all the ingredients for success—good sunshine, no wind, bright-colored tables set up around the pool. Everything was good about the party, or should have been good, except it never quite got off the ground. Perhaps it was the caterers, serving chicken salad in scooped-out fresh pineapples halves, then passing daintily iced petits fours —when all you ever had for dessert at a Pom Pom luncheon was brownies. Everything was done on a scale a bit too elegant for the Pom Poms' comfort.

People walked, instead of running, around the pool. Those playing in the pool laughed, instead of shouting.

Cathy got in line for the diving board. "Coming in?" she asked Deedee.

"No, thanks. I think I'll just sun." Deedee flopped down on one of the chaise longues.

"Come on," Cathy called to Mary Ann. "Let's go."

"Plunge!" Mary Ann jumped off the side of the pool.

They swam two lengths, then paused to rest. Mary Ann's face beamed. Water trickled down her cheeks. Cathy noted a few freckles across her nose.

"Hey, I never noticed your freckles before."

"They only come out in the summer. Aren't they awful?" Mary Ann replied. Then, without waiting for an answer, she gazed around. "Boy, if I lived here, I'd stay home all day every day and just swim and sun. Isn't it the greatest?"

When it came time to go home, everyone thanked Allyson and she accepted their acknowledgments in a regal, slightly bored manner. When it came Cathy's turn to say good-bye, Allyson smiled stiffly.

On the way home Deedee was quiet.

But Mary Ann was bubbling. "Wasn't that the *most*? Gee, it was fun seeing how people like that live."

Deedee sighed. "The whole thing was enough to make you consider turning Communist. You know, the share the wealth bit—"

"You didn't have a good time?" Mary Ann asked.

"Not particularly," Deedee shrugged. "Did you?"

"Sure. I thought it was fantastic."

"Why?"

"Why not?" Mary Ann answered simply.

That was Mary Ann's outlook on life. "Why not?" She accepted her lot with a resignation which armored her against things like petty jealousy. Or perhaps she'd already suffered such grief that jealousy was too trifling an emotion to bother with. Anyway, Mary Ann seemed able to grab moments of happiness here and there, like a child being offered a bag of jelly beans.

"I'm still jazzed," Mary Ann wiggled her toes in her open sandals. "Hey, let's all go to the beach."

Deedee removed her sunglasses. "No, thanks. I'm going home and sulk."

"Aw, come on," Mary Ann said.

Deedee shook her head.

Cathy knew that when Deedee got in one of her moods, there was nothing to do but leave her alone. "O.K., we'll let you off. Then we'll go," she said.

When they were alone, Mary Ann turned to her.

"You know, if it weren't for our living in a little suburb where everybody knows everybody, we'd never have the chance to get inside a place like Allyson's."

Cathy, in no mood to be kind, replied, "And if it weren't for Allyson being kicked out of private school and having to go to Arlington High, we still wouldn't have the chance."

"You can't say it like that, Cathy. You don't know why Allyson was kicked out. Maybe there was a reason."

Cathy laughed. "There was a reason all right."

"But you don't know what it was. So how can you judge?"

"Oh, come on," Cathy said.

Mary Ann seemed anxious to please. "Anyway, if I had a choice between being Allyson Troy or you, I'd be you, Cathy. You *really* have everything."

Cathy's hands felt sticky against the steering wheel. Darn Deedee! Why did she back out on coming to the beach? No. No use blaming Deedee. She never should have allowed Mary Ann to talk her into coming in the first place.

The sun was brighter than ever when they reached the beach. Clumps of picnickers dotted the sand. Fathers built pyramids of driftwood to start fires to which they would later add charcoal and grill hamburgers. Mothers unwrapped hard-boiled eggs and searched for the salt. And a few children, up to their waists in the icy waters of the Pacific, called out, "Aw, it's not cold!" Their voices floated out across the beach and were lost in the sound of the surf.

This was Saturday afternoon in the Bay Area.

Later, these people would pack up, go home to watch television, or play dominoes with the neighbors, or perhaps put on their heavy coats and go to Candlestick Park to see the Giants play ball. Riding a cable car and viewing the Golden Gate Bridge from the top of a hotel was for tourists. This was the San Francisco Bay Area Cathy knew and loved. These were the things she'd miss the most when she went to Virginia.

Cathy and Mary Ann, having found one sandy beach towel in the trunk of the car, walked across the beach.

"Gosh, we should have changed into something grubbier," Cathy said. They spread the towel on the sand and sat down in their good dresses. They were silent for a long time, in the way the ocean makes people silent, so as not to scatter its majesty with words.

Then Mary Ann poked her. "Hey, looky there!"

Cathy turned. Two figures with long hair and short, cut-off jeans were approaching. She wasn't sure at first because of the beard, but from a distance one looked like Jacques, Paul's brother. His companion, the shorter of the two, and beardless, gave you that crazy is-it-a-boy-or-a-girl feeling because of his long wavy hair. When they came closer, she could see that it was indeed Jacques. And his friend, in spite of his hair, was a squat, thick-muscled, well-tanned hippie.

Jacques recognized her at once. "Hey, I know

128

you. You're little Cathy Shorer, Dean Shorer's daughter."

Jacques was taller than Paul, better looking, actually. In spite of his mighty beard, he was quite handsome, in a bland sort of way.

"You're Deedee Wyman's friend, aren't you?" Jacques turned to his companion. "Deedee's my kid brother's girl." His lips puckered in a silent whistle, and his hands traced the female form in the air.

"Hello, Jacques," Cathy said finally. Jacques lived in a world from which ordinary people like herself were cut off, so it was always hard to think of anything to say.

"Gosh, I haven't seen you in a long time, kid. You've really grown up." Then pointing to his friend, he said, "This is Spider."

"How do you do, Spider. This is my friend, Mary Ann Connolly. Mary Ann, this is Jacques Gerow." But all the while she was making introductions, Cathy was aware of Spider taking in Mary Ann's white piqué dress, her suntanned legs and her turquoise sandals.

Spider stuck out his hand to Mary Ann. "Warren Campbell's the name. They call me Spider, for short."

Mary Ann took his hand.

How could she? Cathy thought.

Mary Ann put on a new air for him, gentle, graceful, coy. "I like Spider better than Warren," she said.

129

Spider stared at Mary Ann intently, as though exciting things were going on in his mind.

Cathy gave both the boys what she hoped was a dampening look and stood up. "We were just going."

"What's the hurry?" Spider said, never taking his eyes from Mary Ann.

Cathy leaned over, careful to hold her dress down in the back. "Mary Ann, if you'll get off the towel."

"Oh? Sorry." Mary Ann stood up.

"Like I said, we were just going." Cathy shook sand from the towel and began to fold it.

"Like I said, what's the hurry?" Spider's eyes challenged Cathy.

Jacques, standing to one side like some sort of biblical figure, was amused. "You don't get the message, Spider. The ladies want to go. Now be a gentleman."

Cathy felt the blood rush to her face. "It was good to see you again, Jacques," she said properly, then turned and walked away. Mary Ann followed.

Once in the car they drove away quickly.

"If you wanted to stay, you could have said so, Mary Ann. I mean, we didn't have to leave just because I—"

"No. That's O.K." Mary Ann spoke like someone in a trance.

"Well, the way that creep was looking at you—"

"He looked like a creep because of his hair. But when he got close, did you notice his eyes?"

"No. What about his eyes?"

"They were very nice, somehow." Mary Ann said dreamily.

Mary Ann Connolly was, as Deedee would say, not quite "couth," Cathy thought to herself.

CHAPTER 10

It started as a trickle of gossip, then mushroomed into full-blown scandal.

The same day the Pom Poms had their afternoon party at Allyson's house, Allyson had a night party all of her own. Most of the garbled versions making the rounds claimed not only that "things" were going on in the cabanas, but speed and some lesser drugs were being freely dispensed to the guests. The rumpus started, typically enough, in the rumpus room. Several boys (never identified) crashed chairs through the plate glass sliding doors and upended the Ping-pong table into the Troy's swimming pool. Then, brandishing weapons removed from the wall of the rumpus room—mementos acquired by Mr. Troy on a recent safari in Africa—the boys threatened the life of the housekeeper. The poor woman had locked herself in the library and called the police.

By the time the story was generally known, Todd was defending himself. He claimed he had taken off in his V.W. as the Ping-pong table was being dragged across the broken glass on the terrace to its final resting place, the pool. Not a moment too soon either, because the police car had met Todd on the driveway leading up to the Troy residence. Todd was stopped briefly, but after warning the officers that terrible things were happening "up there," he was allowed to go on his way.

Two things were certain. No charges for damages were being pressed against those involved. And nothing—not a word—appeared in the local paper. People speculated that Mr. Troy's failure to press charges did not attest to his generosity, but to his hope to keep the whole story out of the papers. (It was all over Arlington High, which was almost the same as in the paper, anyway.)

Allyson Troy was white-faced and silent that second week before graduation, and so were a lot of other kids. Todd no longer ate at Allyson's table in the cafeteria, and the crowd at the Malt Shop after school dwindled to the non-swinging group.

Then, two days later, just when things were beginning to calm down, a small item appeared in one of the San Francisco papers. In a Chit-Chat column, of all places!

What daughter of what financial tycoon has her name on a police blotter—along with the names of

*some of her well-heeled friends—for possession of
drugs and immoral acts alleged to have taken place
on the premises of said tycoon's palatial home?*

"The cabanas!" Deedee shrieked. "I told you.
And know what else I heard? It wasn't all going on
in the privacy of the cabanas either. Some of it
was right out in the open—right in the rumpus
room, if you'll pardon the expression. Right where
everybody could see!"

"Deedee, you don't know that's true," Cathy said.

"I don't know it's not true, either," Deedee insisted. "Leave it to Todd, though. He got himself
out before the real fireworks started. He's a cool
cat, that Todd."

She and Deedee were sitting together in the
auditorium waiting to be fitted for their caps and
gowns. It was then that Deedee dropped the un-
settling news about Mary Ann. "Hey, did you know
Mary Ann Connolly went out with a hippie friend of
Paul's brother? Some guy named Spider or something."

Cathy had a sudden sick feeling in the pit of her
stomach. "Oh, no."

"What's the matter?"

"Nothing. We met this Spider and Jacques at the
beach last Saturday. And he's such a creep."

"Well, you can't be responsible for Mary Ann's
boyfriends," Deedee said philosophically. "Besides,
look at what the so-called nice people do. I mean,
who can criticize the hippies? They're tame com-
pared to—" Deedee stopped, staring at a point

above Cathy's head. "Well, speak of the devil!" she said.

Cathy turned. Todd Dillon stood grinning down at both of them.

"Hi!" Todd moved in. "What are you two chicks doing?"

"Nothing." Deedee stood up and quickly disappeared, leaving Cathy and Todd alone.

Todd sat down next to Cathy. "Boy, this cap and gown bit is some drag, isn't it?"

Cathy nodded.

"Cathy, how about you and me going to Grad Night Dance together?" he said. Just like that.

Cathy blinked, taking a moment for her mind to click into place. Of course, with Allyson now tarnished, there was good old Cathy Shorer. She was, if nothing else, safe.

"I think we ought to, don't you?" he asked smoothly.

"I don't think we 'ought to' anything, Todd."

He spread his hands in an "oh that" gesture. "So do you have any plans for Grad Night?"

"As a matter of fact, I do. I was planning on asking my cousin. He lives in the City." Actually, this was the first she'd thought of her cousin. The idea just popped into her mind. But it was a good idea and it would please her mother.

Todd stood up. "O.K., O.K.," he said, like he'd made a good try anyway.

Cathy felt a mixture of anger and admiration for Todd Dillon. The nerve! After all that had happened! But, she thought with a cooler part of her mind, Todd kept *his* nose clean, and he didn't go into a deep blue funk about things in the past. He didn't even go into a pale blue funk! She could learn things from Todd.

Deedee and Paul came over then and sat down. The conversation was nice and general, and pointless and boring; so pretty soon they left. She looked at the back of Paul's neck as they walked away, the way his dark hair grew down to a point.

It took forever to get everybody measured, so they all had to sit and wait their turn. The auditorium was hot and stuffy, and Cathy tried to study to pass the time, but her head throbbed like a giant pulse. She held her history book closer, honestly trying to concentrate, which was probably why she didn't even see Paul slide into the seat next to her.

"Cath?" he said tentatively.

She looked around, careful to make her face blank.

"Is there some place we could talk?"

"I suppose so. If you and Deedee—"

"I mean you and me."

She remained cool. "Why not right here?"

She waited, but Paul seemed to be having trouble finding words. "I mean, some place alone."

She answered him carefully, thoughtfully, and with what she considered later, just the right objective touch.

"Paul, honestly, that's all we've done is talk, ever since this whole thing started. And I don't think these . . . long discussions . . . well, they just make things worse. Deedee told me how you both feel . . ."

"I didn't want to talk about Deedee. I wanted to talk about us."

That stopped her dead.

"I want to apologize for what happened at the beach the other day," he continued.

"Oh that, for heaven's sake!"

"I know you think I was just feeling sorry for you—"

"I understand, honest."

"Look, quit interrupting, will you?"

She couldn't take her eyes off his face, which was coloring faintly.

"I want you to know I wasn't just feeling sorry for you. For me at least, that wasn't it. I tried to pretend at the time that's all it was. But later—"

She cut him off with a laugh. "You've got it backwards, Paul. I should apologize to you, for using your shoulder to cry on. I mean, you're not as good as a psychiatrist, but you're cheaper."

That stopped him dead.

He walked away, looking as though somebody had taken a punch at his soul.

Cathy, feeling lightheaded and dizzy, leaned forward, resting her forehead on the seat in front of her. When she straightened up, Paul was nowhere in sight.

"Nice shot, Straight Arrow," she cried silently. She had dreamed a million times that Paul would come to her; and she had dreamed a million endings—none of them like this. But she always knew if it ever really happened, she'd end it in the cold, brutal way she just had. By not hurting one person, you hurt another. Always a winner, always a loser. God forgive us all.

She guessed she'd reached a new plateau—or maybe it was a hole, the bottom of a hole. Anyway, nothing mattered. Absolutely nothing mattered any more.

So it took practically no effort whatsoever to walk over to Todd and say, "Hey, does the offer still stand for Grad Night?"

"Sure, Cath."

"O.K., you've got yourself a date."

He gulped. "One thing I gotta say for you, kiddo. You're unpredictable."

"I never claimed to be predictable, did I?" She flipped her hair back.

He laughed.

So. It would make her mother happy. And she'd kept her promise to Deedee. Paul, she didn't dare think about.

That night, lying in bed, she thought about her speech to Deedee, the one about having to do whatever it was inside told her to. Big deal. What did she mean by "inside"? Hearing voices? Like she was some kind of Joan of Arc? She didn't understand it herself, so how could she explain the whole thing to Deedee in such positive terms? The thing "inside" made her give Mary Ann the clothes, get her into Pom Poms, disapprove when Mary Ann dated a hippie, and keep on trying to help her.

But was that what she was really trying to do? Just maybe she was trying to make herself feel better—or less awful. Or, as Deedee suggested, maybe it was a form of self-torture. Whatever it was, it was leading her no place. There was nothing she could do that would actually count. She'd just have to give up; blank her mind, like a Yogi; make Mary Ann Connolly a nothing, a zero, a non-exist.

Then, across town, she heard the wail of a siren. That's how it was the night of the accident. The ambulance came, picked up the bodies, and the siren screamed like that.

How could she blank her ears too? There would always be sounds.

She slept for an hour or two, maybe more. But sometime that night she sat bolt upright, with a strange prickling, like cold fingers playing at the back of her neck. She flipped her legs over the side of the bed. She had a funny, disassociated floating feeling, as though she was dreaming. She turned on the bedside light, got up, drank a glass of water, all to prove she was wide-awake. But that eerie feeling wouldn't go away, and she was having that same dream about Mary Ann, only this time she was awake. She remembered, clearly now, the details of the crazy dream, the wind stinging her back, the fog swirling around her face, the screech of brakes as the truck came at Mary Ann. It was like watching a movie for the second time and noticing the little details you missed the first time around.

And she knew, without having to figure it out, that she had to keep on trying to help Mary Ann. There was something yet to do. The knowledge was all dished up to her without reason. It was just there. It was—spooky.

Sleep on it, she told herself. Maybe you'll get some real answers. But the next morning there were no answers, nor the next day, nor the rest of that week.

Graduation came and went. And with it, Paul.

Her mother's hopes were revived when she heard Todd and Cathy were going to Grad Night together. But her Mom got the idea Cathy was less than enthusiastic when she failed to go on the usual diet the week before the dance. For graduation, her parents gave her a gold charm with a wise owl carved of green jade encrusted on it. It was beautiful. Her mother cried when she saw Cathy marching down the aisle. Mary Ann gave Cathy a bottle of cologne, and Cathy cried.

Grad Night was nothing but long. Long. Long. The dance didn't end till two, and then a bunch of kids went to the beach. But Todd and Cathy skipped that part. Todd had sent her an orchid corsage, and the whole evening went smoothly. They didn't talk, they visited, like two strangers waiting at an airport for different planes.

Being graduation, it was an evening of farewells,

with boys cutting in, like they used to back in dancing school days. The only bad moment came when Paul cut in on her. The minute they started to dance Cathy knew it wasn't going to be easy, because with Paul's hand touching hers, it made it eighteen times harder to play it cool.

"You leave tomorrow, huh?" Cathy said.

"Yep. Uncle Sam owns me from now on—for two years, anyway."

"You'll probably snow the girls in your uniform."

He shrugged. "Well, like they say, the uniform makes the man."

They ran out of small talk then, so they just danced, which was better. Or worse, depending on how you looked at it, because the band played a slow song and their heads were touching. Paul's hands tightened around her waist, and she had to fight to keep from getting that same feeling she'd had the day at the beach.

Finally, in that peculiar way Paul had of knowing things, he said, "It'll be better in the fall, when you go to Virginia."

"I know it will, Paul."

The music ended. They started back to the table and Paul said, with a little laugh, "Well, this is it, I guess."

"Yeah, I guess it is."

He smiled and Cathy smiled, but it seemed she should say something more. "Hey, send me your address. I'll . . . bake you some cookies. Or knit you some socks."

"That'll be the day!" He squeezed her hand. " 'Bye, Cath."

He turned to go.

"Paul?" she called after him.

He stopped, came back, and for a moment their fingers touched. "Listen, don't do anything dumb ... like ... well, like getting killed or anything, huh?"

He laughed and walked away.

That's when Grad Night ended. For Cathy at least.

CHAPTER 11

Summer was a letdown. None of the jobs Cathy applied for came through, so she was stuck with a lot of time on her hands. Deedee got a job at the Rec Center, playing games with preschoolers from nine to twelve in the morning. Deedee never mentioned Paul, but Cathy supposed she was hearing from him. Paul sent Cathy a post card with his San Diego address, nothing more. She didn't mention the card to Deedee.

Corny as it was, she started knitting Paul a pair of socks, though she knew she'd never send them. But she had to do something, and writing would be against the rules.

So Cathy was really surprised when Deedee began to date Renny Van Buren. Renny was four years older than they were, and though they'd known him all their lives, he was like another generation. Renny had graduated from college back East in June, and, as Deedee put it, he had "taken a pad in the City." Cathy thought pad was the wrong word. A fellow like Renny would have "quarters." But she didn't say that to Deedee.

"Would you believe Renny got a wonderful job in a bank?" Deedee said in awe.

"I'd believe it," Cathy answered.

Deedee gave her a funny look. "Well, Renny's just somebody to date," she explained. "We're good friends. He knows all about Paul."

"Boy, you've come up in the world. Dating a big banker—"

Deedee laughed. "I'd rather have Paul buy me a bag of popcorn and go sit in the park."

So that was that.

Now that summer was here, Cathy found it a relief not having to go to school, not having to face Mary Ann, and she began to understand how much just seeing Mary Ann had bugged her. Mary Ann called once and told her Spider had arranged for a coffeehouse in the City to show her paintings, and had sold two during the first week. She was very excited. Cathy tried to match her enthusiasm, but knowing Spider has assumed the roll of Mary Ann's manager, she felt only pity for Mary Ann. For some reason Cathy hated herself more because she felt pity for Mary Ann than because she had hurt her. Pity bound her to Mary Ann like a wet rope.

But Mary Ann was busy painting during the day and seeing Spider at night, so they didn't see each other often. One night Cathy, Mary Ann, and Liz McKneally went to a movie. (Spider gave Mary Ann the night off, Liz whispered confidentally.)

As the days went by, Cathy reached the point where she realized she would never get over the whole thing, but she might, she just might learn to live with it.

On the Fourth of July, Renny got Cathy a blind date with a friend who worked in the bank, and the four of them went to the Spaghetti Factory for dinner and to North Beach afterward. But all the swinging spots in North Beach were no-no's for Deedee and Cathy because they were under twenty-one. After being turned away at the door of three places (it was embarrassing) they walked back to the car. As they passed a fire station, Deedee, in a playful mood, stopped and chattered with the fireman sitting out in front, and eventually the four of them were invited in for coffee. Though they said it was against the rules, the firemen let Deedee and Cathy put on fire hats and climb up in the cab of the fire engine, just to see what it was like. Cathy thought it was fun and Deedee was cracking up with laughter. But the two boys watched them as though observing infants at play. Deedee finally got the message, climbed down, and tried to act more sophisticated. They didn't double date after that.

Cathy's family vacationed at Lake Tahoe the last two weeks in July. Although the house they rented was too small and too far back from the lake, and her mother complained the whole time because she'd wanted them all to drive to Virginia instead, it was, as her father explained, only her mother's usual summer syndrome. To Cathy the vacation was at least a change of irritations.

Things seemed to be settling into a pattern of odds and ends adding up to nothing. All Cathy could think about was getting ready for college, and wondering if September would ever come.

Until the night Mary Ann's grandmother called. It was the night they'd returned from Tahoe, while they were eating dinner, and Cathy stood listening to that good Christian voice while her parents looked on. She felt trapped, Mrs. Connolly's soft voice entangling her like a spider's web.

"Cathy," Mrs. Connolly was saying, "Mary Ann's having her sixteenth birthday Friday, and I thought it would be nice if I had a little party for her. Nothing big, of course. Liz McKneally and her beau. You, and your date. And Spider."

"Spider?"

"Spider Campbell. He's the boy Mary Ann's been seeing lately."

"Yes, I know." She could tell by the way Mrs. Connolly said his name that she didn't approve of Spider either.

"Well, I don't know. You see, I haven't been dating much lately—"

"Oh, that doesn't make any difference. Come yourself. You don't have to bring a boy."

Cathy hesitated. Mrs. Connolly was urging her. "We haven't seen you all summer, Cathy, and you *are* one of Mary Ann's favorites. We'll expect you, and don't worry about not bringing a date."

"Well, thanks, Mrs. Connolly. What time?"

Mrs. Connolly said around six, and Cathy thanked her again and hung up.

"Who was that?" her mother asked, as if she hadn't already heard.

"Mary Ann Connolly's grandmother. She's having a birthday party for her next Friday."

Her mother put down her fork. "Cathy, whatever made you get in with that girl . . . that Connolly girl?"

Cathy feigned bewilderment. "What's the matter with her?"

"Nothing's the matter with her; she just doesn't seem to be your type."

"Oh, come on, Mom." Cathy pushed away the dinner plate and started on the strawberry short-cake.

"Finish your dinner first."

So she went back to the meat loaf, wondering whose type anybody was. And did people really come in types like shoes came in sizes? And would the hurt inside her ever go away?

The following Friday night the fog came in early, turning the sky the color of lead. The wind ate through to the bones, and by the time Cathy arrived at Mary Ann's her hair was a mess. She walked up the front steps with the record album all wrapped up in blue paper, feeling as though she were stepping back onto an old treadmill.

"Hi!" Mary Ann seemed so pleased to see her.

"Happy birthday, kiddo."

Mary Ann was wearing the blue knit outfit she'd sent her. It gave Cathy a start somehow.

Mary Ann took Cathy into the living room. "You remember Spider, don't you?"

Spider grunted a greeting. While Mary Ann was unwrapping the record, Cathy took a good look at him. He'd cut his hair so that now he merely looked untidy instead of nauseous.

Mrs. Connolly came in from the kitchen, all smiles. Even in a pink dress and frilly apron, she still looked like a nurse.

"How nice of you to come, Cathy!" Mrs. Connolly acted surprised—as if Cathy had dropped in from nowhere and she hadn't been the one to invite her in the first place. "Liz and her boyfriend couldn't come, so there'll be just the four of us." Then she spied the record. "Oh, you shouldn't have . . . let me have your coat, dear . . . Mary Ann, take Cathy's coat . . . we'll have supper in just a minute . . . Mary Ann, you come help."

Cathy guessed that the reason Mrs. Connolly was talking so much was because she was nervous. Which made two of them. Cathy started toward the kitchen, but Mrs. Connolly put out her hand.

"No, dear, you and Spider sit and visit. We'll be ready as soon as I toss the salad."

Cathy sat at one end of the sofa, Spider at the

other. He pulled out a cigarette, lit it and flipped the burned match squarely on the coffee table.

That figures, Cathy thought. She pushed an ash tray toward him.

As Spider gave her a long look of appraisal, he said, "Mary Ann's glad you came."

Cathy nodded. "We're good friends."

"Yeah." He shifted his squat legs under the low coffee table. "She's had a rough time. She still does, for that matter."

For a minute she didn't follow him.

"You know . . . the phone call . . . the accident," he explained.

If there was one thing Cathy didn't want to discuss with Spider Campbell, it was the accident.

"You live around here, Spider?" She changed the subject.

"No. In the City."

She was about to ask how he'd located Mary Ann, after that day at the beach, then thought she'd better not.

As if reading her mind, he said, "Jacques called his kid brother and got Mary Ann's address and phone number for me. Then when I found out about her painting, I took some pictures up to Coffee and Conversation. Gus, the owner, is a friend of mine. He's sold quite a few for her."

"That's nice," Cathy commented.

"Coffee and Conversation is a real tourist trap, you know."

"No, I didn't. I don't get up to . . . that part of town often."

"It's not where the real swingers hang out."

I'll bet you're an authority on that, Cathy thought grimly. There was something about the way Spider was looking at her that gave her the creeps. It wasn't an admiring look, or anything close to it. It was . . . almost as though he knew a secret she didn't know.

"Mary Ann told me about the clothes you gave her after the accident," he said in a new tone.

She nodded dumbly.

Restlessly he got up, moved to the window. "She's gotta find out who made that phone call. She's gotta find out, somehow." He turned, observing her closely.

Mrs. Connolly stuck her head into the living room. "Supper's ready."

Cathy stood up, not looking at Spider, and walked into the dining room. Seated at the table, she didn't remember what was said at first, because she was enveloped in a cold blanket of terror, and was aware only of the instinct to survive. She made no effort to follow the conversation; she only groped with the growing feeling that she had walked into a trap.

The main thing—and she kept concentrating on it—was not to spill the spaghetti. Somehow that would be the end, the dead giveaway. But the spaghetti was as slippery as her fingers, so she pushed it back and forth on the plate, hoping no one would notice.

Then, to her horror, Spider began to talk in a fixed, calculating tone about the night of the phone call. "What did the person say to Mary Ann's mother, Mrs. Connolly? That someone *tried* to attack her, or that someone *had* attacked her?"

Mrs. Connolly's face went white. "I don't remember, Spider."

Mary Ann had a piece of lettuce, speared on a fork, halfway to her mouth. The fork dropped to the plate, splashing dressing on the white tablecloth like a tiny Roman candle.

"Didn't the police even try to track down the phone call? It's just possible it wasn't a joke. Maybe it was for real and somebody *was* attacked, and, in the excitement, dialed the wrong number?"

Spider looked across the table at Cathy. His mouth was grim, but way down deep, behind his eyes, she got the impression he was laughing.

He knows. He knows and is trying to trap me. He's trying to find some way to make it easier for me to tell—providing me with an excuse. But he's going to force me to tell.

The air turned clammy and thick and her body seemed forced back into the chair, as though a seat belt chained her in place.

Then there came a cry of pain from Mary Ann, just a little whimper you could barely hear, and she pushed away from the table and ran from the room.

"That's just something we don't discuss, Spider," Mrs. Connolly was half-wailing, half-crying.

Cathy was having a hard time with her hands. She kept telling herself to hold on, keep them folded in her lap.

"Sorry," Spider mumbled.

But he didn't seem sorry. He seemed like a lawyer in a court scene about to make his point. Mrs. Connolly swept into the bedroom after Mary Ann, leaving Spider and Cathy looking at each other.

"Things people do in the past shouldn't be held against them, should they?" he said reasonably.

He's playing cat-and-mouse with me.

"A person should remain innocent until proven guilty. Isn't that what the Establishment says?" he pressed on.

She had been sentenced. There was no appeal. Her lips began to tremble like a pair of butterflies attached to her mouth, no part of her at all. Instinct told her to get out now, because in about one minute she was going to crack up.

"You ought to have more sense!" She pushed away from the table. But her words carried no conviction because her voice trembled like a small, harmless rumble of thunder.

Spider leaned back in his chair, satisfied at last. "I know what her grandmother thinks," he announced quietly.

She knew she ought to answer. Silence would indict her. Her mind teemed with answers, but she only said, "You've—you've spoiled Mary Ann's birthday!" She blurted out the words, but another part of her brain was working. All right, he'd caught her off-balance. Did he knew for sure, or did he only suspect? Did Mrs. Connolly know too? Did they both know? And the only one who didn't know was Mary Ann, so they had gotten her here because they wanted her to tell Mary Ann?

This was the living end. There was nothing left to do, so she scrambled for the front closet, grabbed her coat and cried, "Tell them I had to leave."

Then she ran. Out the front door, down the steps and into the car. Jamming the key in the ignition, the motor roared and died. She'd flooded the engine. The front porch light flashed on, outlining Spider in the doorway. She was doomed. She gunned the engine, burned the tires and, thankfully, the car tore away.

The house was dark except for the blue light from the television in the living room. She tried to slip quietly in the front door but her mother must have sensed something wrong. She got up from the sofa. "Is that you, Cathy? What's the matter?"

It took a long time to get her breath. "Nothing . . . Mary Ann got sick . . . and it broke up . . . everything."

"Oh." Her mother returned to the sofa and Cathy escaped upstairs.

She was so frightened that she couldn't sit, she couldn't do anything but walk back and forth and peer out the bedroom window. Any minute she expected to see a car drive up—with Spider and Mrs. Connolly, maybe even the police. How had Spider guessed? Or maybe he hadn't. Maybe he was still putting two and two together.

Todd's words came back to her. "You keep fooling around with that girl, and pretty soon the beans are going to spill all over the place." Todd was right. Deedee was right. Paul? Oh, God, how she wished she could talk to Paul.

"Oh, Paul, please. I need you so," she sobbed out loud.

This was getting her no place. She fumbled in her desk and found Paul's post card. Suppose she called him in San Diego? She had the address; would that be enough? No, the phone was in the living room, and her mother wouldn't leave the TV until the late show was over. Maybe she could get to a phone booth. She searched her purse. Two dollars. Oh, God, she had to find more money. Dad's wallet? No, it was still early; he was probably in bed reading. She fumbled through three other purses and finally found another dollar bill in her white evening bag. Three dollars; that ought to do it.

She slipped downstairs and out the back door, afraid to take the car for fear her mother would hear. She ran the two blocks to the filling station. Tearing down the street, she realized she was running through the fog without her coat. She had a weird feeling she'd been through this before, and it was happening all over again. She stopped, panting for breath. She *had* been through this before—running through the fog like this. In the dream!

At the filling station she got change, rushed to the phone booth, put in a dime and dialed the operator. She looked at her watch. It was eight-twenty.

At eight-thirty they located Paul, so it was a good thing she'd called person to person.

"Deposit two dollars and five cents for three minutes," the operator said.

She was so shaken that she had a hard time adding up the correct change. "Paul? It's me. Cathy."

"What's the matter?" He was instantly alert.

"I think they know."

"Who knows? What are you talking about?"

"I think Mary Ann's boyfriend *knows*—about me."

There was a long silence, then a low whistle. "Are you sure?"

"No, but I think he does."

"Who's Mary Ann's boyfriend? Not that friend of Jacques?"

"Yes. Spider Campbell."

"Oh, God, that's *my* fault!" He sighed. "Look, try to tell me from the beginning."

She took a deep breath and started talking, but she was so frightened, she obviously wasn't making sense, because Paul kept interrupting, trying to get the story straight.

"Your three minutes are up. Please signal when you are through."

"Operator, how much is another three minutes?" she asked.

"Twenty-five cents a minute, plus tax."

"All right. Signal me when three more minutes are up. Paul, I can't talk any longer than that. I don't have enough money."

"You're just scared, Cath. This Spider guy is suspicious. He's just fishing."

"He *knows,* I can tell. He's trying to force me—"

"He doesn't know. You've just hit the panic button. Look, if it would do any good, I'd say tell them, tell the whole world. But what would that accomplish? It'd cause you trouble, and we'd only hurt Mary Ann all over again."

"I know. I know. But what if she finds out?"

"She won't. Not if you don't crack up."

"But what if Spider already knows? Maybe he's even told Mrs. Connolly. Or maybe not. Maybe *she* knows and has told Spider. He told me. He said he knows what her grandmother thinks!"

"For Pete's sake, she wouldn't invite you to the house if she knew. That doesn't make sense."

"Not unless they're trying to trap me. They don't want to tell Mary Ann. They're trying to make *me* do it. Oh, Paul, I need you," she cried.

"The whole thing's been killing you ever since it happened. I don't know, Cath. Sometimes I think you ought to tell them. For your own sake—"

"Your three minutes are up."

So was her money.

"Good-bye, Paul." She hung up.

CHAPTER 12

Somehow she got back home, even got to bed. It was a long, quiet night. The ticking of the grandfather clock downstairs seemed to be the only sound in the world. It was so deadly quiet, her breathing rattled the stillness of the room. She'd read once about being in the eye of a hurricane, how absolutely still it is, and she thought, "This is the way it must be."

She awoke with no sense of time having passed. Her mother was shaking her, forcing her to open her eyes. And when she did, at once the room was filled with sunlight, so she closed her eyes again.

"Cathy, it's Mary Ann's grandmother. She says it's important." Her mother shook her harder. "Get up. You'll have to talk to her. I told her Mary Ann wasn't here, but she's awfully upset."

It took Cathy a moment to get with it. "Mary Ann—here?"

"Cathy, she's waiting on the phone. Just talk to her. I can't make sense out of the woman. Now hurry."

Cathy stumbled downstairs in her bare feet, alternating between fear and despair. The receiver was off the hook, lying on the desk, and her victim —her random victim—was waiting. Or was Cathy herself the random victim? It was hard to tell any more.

"Mrs. Connolly?"

"She's gone." The words gushed out of the receiver. "Mary Ann's gone. I thought she might have come to you. I don't know what to do now. I think . . . I'll have to call the police."

"Mrs. Connolly—"

"We had an awful scene last night."

"She left last night? With Spider?"

"She's been gone all night. Oh, Cathy, I suppose she's with Spider. I don't know where she is. I finally left, went to my room, and when I came out they were both gone."

Cathy tried to think, but the pieces weren't fitting together. The instinct for self-preservation was still strong, because the one thought she kept clinging to—through the whole disjointed conversation— was the possibility that Mrs. Connolly *didn't* know, after all.

"If she's with Spider, she's probably in the City," Cathy said carefully.

Mrs. Connolly started to cry then, and Cathy was sorry she'd said it.

"Cathy, help me find her."

"I'll try."

"Cathy—" Mrs. Connolly's voice was almost incoherent now. "I tried. God knows, I tried. And you mustn't blame Mary Ann either. She didn't mean any harm. It was just kid stuff, it always had been . . . sending taxis to my home . . . orders from the Chicken Shack . . . just annoying prank phone calls . . . she didn't mean . . . she had no idea . . . it was just another joke . . . she didn't think we'd really believe . . ."

"What are you saying, Mrs. Connolly?"

"I tried to forgive her. God knows, I tried."

"Forgive her for what?"

"For making the phone call."

"Mrs. Connolly—"

"I never told a soul. That's what I promised the night of the accident, and I kept that promise. I didn't want Mary Ann to suffer the rest of her life . . . I gave her a home . . . she always denied making the phone call, but she *knew* I knew . . . so it wasn't easy, living together. Then that miserable Spider came along. She was looking for sympathy, I suppose. So she told her story to him. To him, of all people! She was always so afraid you, her friends, *anybody* would find out!" Her voice broke. "She must be up there in San Francisco with those—those hippies."

161

"You mean . . . all this time . . . you've been blaming Mary Ann?"

"I haven't been blaming her. I've protected her. That's what I tried to tell Spider. You must understand. I've tried to forgive—"

Cathy felt as though she'd come to the end of a long journey, and now she knew why.

"Mrs. Connolly, you'd better get hold of yourself, because I have something important to tell you. Mary Ann didn't make that phone call."

Complete silence on the other end of the line. And Cathy thought, *What a lousy way to have to tell her—over the phone.* It started over the phone, so maybe that's the way it had to end—over the phone.

Still Mrs. Connolly hadn't spoken.

"Did you hear me, Mrs. Connolly? Mary Ann didn't make that phone call. I did."

The silence was unbearable. It went on and on, like the end of the world. Then Cathy hung up and just stood there, staring at the phone. It looked just like it did the night she'd made the phone call. It looked alive.

Her mother was in the kitchen.

"Can I have the car?"

"What for?"

"Please don't ask, Mom." Cathy stepped to the kitchen doorway. "I've just got to have the car. I've got to find Mary Ann. Then I'll tell you everything, and you'll hate it. You'll hate me."

Her mother started to protest, then stopped. She

must have sensed something awfully wrong because she opened her purse and handed Cathy the keys without a word.

Driving on the freeway, Cathy tried to arrange her thoughts. Put first things first: find Mary Ann. The rest, the lives she had wrecked, the suffering— she'd think of all that later. Not just yet.

Coffee and Conversation, where Mary Ann sold her paintings, was a good place to start. The freeway, so straight and uncluttered this time of the morning, had a hypnotic effect on Cathy, and her mind spilled over to the other. It all fitted so perfectly now—the way Mary Ann called her grandmother "Mrs. Connolly," and Mary Ann's vague remarks—"I used to be a brat to her . . . she took the three to eleven shift so we wouldn't have to see each other . . ." Then Spider, last night, "I know what her grandmother thinks."

She kept seeing pictures in her mind. Mary Ann, living all those months with the good Christian woman who kept trying to understand and forgive. And Mary Ann could do nothing to prove her innocence. She could do nothing but keep on living with that terrible Christian forgiveness.

". . . sending taxis to my home . . . just annoying prank phone calls . . ." Then the one big phone call came in, and Mary Ann got hung with it!

Hadn't she sensed something like this all along? Was this the "thing inside" that kept pushing her on, the nagging sense of unfinished business that kept tormenting her, the dream she dreamed even when she was awake? It had all led to this moment; and now she had to save Mary Ann—Mary Ann, who, from the beginning, had been her random victim.

She'd been to hippie-land with the kids before, just for kicks. The district was confined to several blocks of the City, and she'd always thought of it as a very small area. But now the site appeared to be one, huge carnival. They were having a Be-In, the banner stretched across the street proclaimed. So many people were milling in the street, she couldn't get near in the car, so she had to go back and park several blocks away. She stopped at a filling station to look up Coffee and Conversation in the phone book. There was no listing.

So she started walking. The street oozed with people, most of them all dressed up in strange costumes—Indian headbands, blankets—like kids playing dress-up. A tall boy wrapped in a blanket, wearing a tiny mirror strapped to his forehead, blocked her way.

"Be, baby, be." He touched her face with a long fingernail. Cathy shuddered and backed away.

She found herself face to face with a pretty girl, long blonde hair cascading to her shoulders.

"Could you help me, please? Do you know a place called Coffee and Conversation?"

The girl handed Cathy a white paper rose and her lips moved in a whisper. "Given in love," was all that Cathy heard. The girl turned and continued passing out paper roses.

She spied a lone man leaning against a building. When she got closer, she saw he was only a teenager, trying to grow a beard His hair was long, stringy. and he wore an earring in one ear.

"Please help me. I'm looking for someone."

"Tried the Switchboard?"

"No, what's the Switchboard?"

"At the end of the block. on the right. It's a place where you leave messages."

"Thank you " She hurried to the end of the block and entered the old frame house Inside, a long hall painted green stretched the length of the building. To her left stood a card table and an empty chair. A middle-aged man in a white coat—she thought he might be a doctor—stepped from one of the doors into the hall.

She ran to him. "Excuse me, could you help? I'm looking for a place called Coffee and Conversation."

"Coffee and Conversation? Never heard of it. They change all the time. you know." He gave Cathy a professional look. "What are you doing here, young lady?"

"I'm looking for someone. Mary Ann Connolly. I think I can find her through Coffee and Conversation, and a man named Gus. She used to sell paintings there."

"You look straight," he noted mildly, as though checking a list of symptoms.

"Please. I'm trying to find someone."

He gestured with his head. "There's a bulletin

board at the end of the hall. You can leave a message."

"Thank you." She ran down the hall.

"Hey," he called after her. "Gus, you said? Is he the owner? I think I know the place you're talking about. It's a coffeehouse for tourists. Used to be called The Cellar. On the corner of Ross and Livingston."

"Ross and Livingston. Thank you, thank you very much."

She picked up a pencil and paper and scrawled a note. "Mary Ann Connolly. Call me. Very important. Cathy." She tacked the paper to the bulletin board. But there were so many messages already there, she didn't think Mary Ann would ever find it.

Then she set out for Ross and Livingston.

Coffee and Conversation was on the outskirts of the hippie district, a coffeehouse all made up to look real beat. Gus turned out to be about six-feet-five, with flaming red hair and an enormous paunch. One look and Cathy knew he wasn't beat, either. Gus was a businessman. The place was almost empty, and with sunlight streaming in the front door you could see specks of dust floating in the air. The walls were covered with paintings, each with a little white price tag thumbtacked beneath.

Gus didn't want to talk.

"But it's terribly important. You know her. You've sold her paintings. Mary Ann Connolly, about five-feet-three, light hair—"

"Did you try the Switchboard?"

Cathy nodded. Gus stared at her, and she knew he wasn't giving away information.

"She's run away," Cathy said.

"They've all run away," he replied with a sweep of his hand. "Mary Ann too, huh? Didn't figure that. She was a talented kid. Lots of ambition, not the type—"

"You do know her! Please, it's important. Her grandmother wants her back."

"Grandmothers, mothers, fathers—they all want 'em back. Who knows where they are? Out there, floating around some place."

"Please, Mr. . . . Gus, have you seen Mary Ann last night or today?"

"I don't run a Missing Persons—"

"Just tell me, please. Have you?"

Gus picked up a tray of mugs and moved them behind the bar. "She was in this morning. Picked up some money I owed her. I don't know where she went from here, though."

"Do you know Spider?"

"Yeah, I know Spider."

Was he with her?"

"No, she was alone."

"Where can I start looking?"

"There's a whole Be-In going on in the streets. Why don't you start there?" He chuckled as though he'd made a little joke.

"O.K., but where else?"

"Well," he scratched the back of his neck. "If she's with Spider, you might try The Coffin."

"The Coffin? That's the name of the place?"

"Yeah, it swings twenty-four hours a day. That's where I'd look if she's with Spider. If she's moved in, she might be any place. Any one of the houses."

Cathy found The Coffin. It was in the basement of an old building with only a small, hand-printed sign in front; but you could hear the music all the way out to the sidewalk. She climbed down a long flight of stairs into the noise.

The Coffin was a large, dank room, like a dungeon in a fairy tale. It took a while to adjust to the darkness. At the far end of the basement, a combo played on a makeshift stage while colored psychedelic lights twitched on and off. Behind the microphone, a pretty girl with hair to her waist, head thrown back, eyes closed, swayed like a snake charmer, chanting, "I don't know—I don't care—and it doesn't make any difference." The room vibrated with the music, and all over was the smell of too many bodies too close together. And the sick sweet odor of pot.

There were so many of them, lines of kids, like hedges growing out of the floor. Cathy stumbled from one laughing group to another, searching for Mary Ann's face.

"Share our Love Circle." Someone grabbed her hand and she became part of a grotesque circle going round and round, like little kids playing ring-around-the-rosy.

She bolted and fell, then found herself cowering on her hands and knees trying to fight down the panic in her throat, afraid someone might step on her. It was like a crazy house at a carnival where you keep bumping into mirrors and there is no escape.

Then Cathy saw her. Mary Ann was sitting on a blanket, her legs drawn up under her, looking very small, very out of it. Spider wasn't with her, but two bearded kids shared the blanket on which she was sitting. One, gentle and benign, was strumming a guitar; the other sat so close he touched her, but was staring at a point over her shoulder, unaware she was next to him.

That was the weird thing about the sights and sounds of "sharing." Nobody was sharing anything. Everybody was doing what he was doing by himself.

Cathy stumbled to her feet, pushing people aside. When she reached Mary Ann, she knelt down in front of the blanket. Mary Ann was wearing a button which said, "Am I God's Joke?"

Cathy wanted to die.

Mary Ann smiled, as though she wasn't surprised to see her, and Cathy wondered for a horrible moment if she'd been smoking pot or dropping acid— or any one of a dozen different things people smoked, ate, snuffed, or injected into their veins.

"You shouldn't have come," Mary Ann said simply. Her face was pale like someone who'd been sick a long time.

"I made the phone call, Mary Ann. It was me."

There was no comprehension on Mary Ann's face.

"Your grandmother thought it was you; I just found that out. But it wasn't you, Mary Ann. It was me, Cathy. I made the phone call. It didn't . . . I didn't mean . . . I didn't know . . . but I did it."

Mary Ann wasn't getting the message. She opened her mouth, but no words came out. Cathy reached for her hand, cold and wet, and clung to it.

"I did it. I made the phone call." She kept babbling the words over and over, until Mary Ann could no longer escape their meaning, until she could brand truth on her mind.

Mary Ann tried to speak, but she had no breath. Yet Cathy could tell she was beginning to understand because something like outrage narrowed her eyes. But Mary Ann's hand remained cold, like the hand of a dead person. Then slowly she drew back her arm.

"Can't you say anything, Mary Ann? What's the matter?"

The matter was that Mary Ann was peering at her, trying to replace one image with another. You couldn't blame her. It must have been rough, so rough after all those months, to see her friend, her benefactor, old rah-rah, Pom Pom Cathy—to see that same person now as the one who caused the death of her parents. And then hung her with the blame.

Suddenly Mary Ann jerked her hand to her mouth

and made it into a fist, a quivering wet fist, and Cathy thought she was going to hit her. She wished she would. But then Mary Ann's hand fluttered, went limp, and dropped to her lap.

"Your grandmother wants you home. Please come home, Mary Ann. She knows I made the phone call. She doesn't think it was you any more. Do you understand?"

Finally, Mary Ann answered in a strange husky voice. "I understand."

"Will you come home with me now?"

She shook her head.

"Will you come home? Will you, Mary Ann? Please get out of here." Cathy looked around. "Where's Spider? Will he take you home?"

"Spider left me. I'll get home by myself." There was no expression on her face.

Then it was all over. There was nothing left to do but get up and leave. She couldn't feel better yet. She couldn't feel anything but the craving to get out of the place and crawl away. Maybe later, when she had time to think, she'd feel relief, but she didn't know. Her eyes were still filled with the sight of Mary Ann's blank face and that awful button pinned to her blouse.

"Am I God's Joke?"

CHAPTER 13

Afterward, it was like coming out of an anesthetic. She'd done what had to be done, and from then on she stood back and watched time pass. She would remember only the big crucial moments, and even those she seemed to remember as an observer.

Like telling her parents that night. Her mother wept such a long, long time; and all she could do was sit and wait for her to stop so she could go on explaining. Her father's face stiffened into a block of granite and stayed that way through the whole thing, though every once in a while he'd go over and put his arm around her mother and try to comfort her.

After she'd finished, they kept repeating the same question over and over. "Why didn't you tell us?"

"I was scared to." That was all she could say.

So she started all over again. She tried to explain how it started, with her sick little joke, the phone call. And how, afterward, she had this great compulsion to help Mary Ann, how she could never seem to leave Mary Ann alone. She didn't understand it herself. It was just something she knew she had to do because there was a reason, some place. And now she'd found the reason.

"It was like it *had* to happen," Cathy said.

"What do you mean, it had to happen? I don't understand that kind of talk," her mother cried.

"I don't understand it either," she answered quietly.

They thought her slightly mad; she could tell by the expressions on their faces.

Her mother finally said she was "plagued" by a sense of guilt. That was the whole thing in a nutshell.

There was nothing further Cathy could say.

Her mother stood up, walked to the window. "That poor child," she sobbed.

"Who? Mary Ann?" Cathy hoped she was referring to Mary Ann.

"Yes, Mary Ann," her mother said, then added, "And you too, honey. You too."

Later that night her father drove over to the Connolly's. When he came home he was wiping his head with his handkerchief.

"Mary Ann's home," he announced. And Cathy relaxed for the first time. "Mrs. Connolly notified the police she'd returned. She did call the police, you know." He sat down in his brown leather chair. His face looked gray.

"What did they say, Dad?"

He didn't look at her. "The same thing we said. They just kept asking, 'why?' "

"Oh."

"And there wasn't any answer I could give, Cathy."

Cathy crossed the room and sat at his feet. Her father stroked her hair and just stared into space, saying nothing.

She had to ask it. "Do they hate me a lot?"

He looked down at her, an unbearable sadness on his face. "Not yet. Right now Mrs. Connolly only hates herself for accusing Mary Ann. And Mary Ann—she's getting used to the idea of no longer being the accused. Later, I suppose—when they've had time—they'll hate you."

She shivered and he squeezed her shoulder reassuringly. "Mrs. Connolly agreed they wouldn't tell people the awful part."

The "awful" part meant that Cathy Shorer had made the phone call, she guessed. Or that Mrs. Connolly had believed Mary Ann made the phone call? Was there any part of the whole thing that wasn't awful?

It didn't make the slightest difference as it turned out, because by Monday night the whole story was all over town. So somebody told. Tuesday night, one of the ladies from the Crestwood Garden Club even brought in food, like it was a funeral. It was, in a way. Cathy couldn't eat. She kept wondering if someone had brought food to the Connolly's too.

After dinner she called Deedee and asked her over. Deedee brought a copy of *Stanyan Street* and they read poems aloud in Cathy's room, and Deedee never mentioned Mary Ann. Which was nice.

In fact, everybody was nice to the whole family.

As the days went by her mother said she realized, for the first time, how beloved a man Cathy's father was in this town. People went out of their way to tell him how sorry they were for both families.

Eventually the days began to be divided into mornings, afternoons, and nights. She remembered to wash her hair, pick up her room before Mrs. Young came on Saturdays, so she knew she was coming back into the world. Her mother and father were trying to program her back to normal living. They talked ecstatically about how happy she'd be when she went to college in September, and they kept bugging her to get out of the house, play tennis, do anything.

"You just can't sit here all summer long," her mother kept saying.

But Cathy thought she could.

Then Paul's letter arrived. From Honolulu. He'd heard from Deedee.

". . . about Mary Ann, you cared enough to do

what you thought was right. That's all anyone can ask of you, Cath. Just that you care. I wish I could have been with you, though. You needed me. I think we need each other—we always have. I never did believe all that jazz about me being cheaper than a psychiatrist. What we felt that day on the beach was for real. Maybe, when I get home, I'll get a chance to prove it to you."

She asked Deedee to come over that afternoon, and told her she'd had a letter from Paul.

"It's not exactly news to me," Deedee said. "I heard from him, too."

"Oh, Deedee!"

"No! Please, don't you explain too. So it was over for us a long time ago. Before graduation, even. What we had, the whole thing, went dead. I just refused to bury it."

"How about Renny?"

Deedee gave a philosophical shrug. "Well, one thing you've got to say for Renny, he's *here*, not halfway across the Pacific."

"Deedee, let's go to a movie tomorrow night, huh? It'll be like old times."

It was, almost.

Until after the show, on the way home, driving past the Malt Shop. There were a lot of cars parked in front, and Cathy, knowing she had to take the plunge sooner or later, decided to take it now. Cathy wondered later if Deedee ever knew how much nerve it took to get the words out. But she finally did. "Hey, shall we stop for a coke?"

"I can't," Deedee said too quickly. "I promised I'd be home early, and I've got to wash my hair yet."

So it wasn't going to be like old times, ever. They'd established that. Cathy didn't blame Deedee, really. She should have remembered that Deedee never did like to back a loser.

"Well, 'bye," she said when Deedee dropped her off. She thought that they both knew it was a real good-bye. Too many things had happened. Their friendship ended without a whole lot of explanations, just as it had existed without explanations. One thing she had to say of Deedee, though; she was a lady, right to the end.

When Cathy ran up the front steps, she noticed there was no blue light coming from the TV in the living room. Then she saw her mother and father sitting together on the front porch. She hadn't seen them together like that in a long time. So she sat down on the front steps and leaned against the bannister.

"Did you have a good time?" her mother asked anxiously.

"Yes, sure."

"See, it wasn't so hard once you made up your mind to do it, was it?" her father said.

"No, not so hard." The night was warm, with not a trace of fog.

Her Dad put out his hand. "Come sit with us, Shug."

He hadn't called her Shug—short for Sugar—since she was a child.

But she didn't answer and she didn't move. Her father must have known how she felt because he said, "You're still our little girl, and we still love you."

She closed her eyes. She wasn't anybody's little girl any more, though she wished she were. She opened her eyes then, half-aware of how the old honeysuckle had grown nearly to the roof, and thought how sad it was . . . growing up . . . learning to be cruel. No, she wasn't a little girl any more.

"Was it a good movie?" her mother asked.

"Very good. It ended happily-ever-after."

They didn't answer. Suddenly she was tired of everything, just everything in the whole universe. She wanted to scream or do something! She stared at her parents sitting together, and for the briefest moment she felt resentment toward them. If it hadn't been for them and their being together, she wouldn't have been born and everything would be . . .

She shook the crazy thought out of her head and stood up. "I'm bushed."

"Sure you don't want something to drink? There's iced tea—"

"Good-night, Mom. 'Night, Dad." She kissed them both, like she used to when she was a little girl. It was just a remembrance, really.

The bedroom was hot and stuffy and she opened the window and sat on the floor, staring at the sky. She wondered what Mary Ann was doing tonight, and was surprised to find she could wonder about her almost as if she were anybody else in the world. Which was something.

What would become of Mary Ann? What would become of them all?

Mary Ann would make it, she thought. Mary Ann would accept any joy that happened to come her way, and not ask for seconds. Therein lay her happiness.

Deedee would make it. She would marry someone like Renny, live in a smart little done-over Victorian house in San Francisco, eat lunch at Trader Vic's, and go to the symphony on Thursday afternoons. Which was what Deedee wanted.

Todd, no doubt, would maneuver his way into being a three-star general. Maybe even a four-star one!

For herself, for Paul, she didn't know. She got out Paul's letter and read it for the hundredth time. ". . . you cared enough to do what you thought was right. That's all anyone can ask of you, Cath. Just that you care. . . ." And she thought that if everything worked out right, just exactly right, and someday she married Paul, maybe she'd learned enough to be a good wife to him. A really good wife.

She put his letter back in the envelope. You can endure anything, she decided, if you only have something to look forward to. And she had Paul's coming home to look forward to.

Then she put his letter back in the desk and went to bed.

ABOUT THE AUTHOR

EDITH MAXWELL is married to a San Francisco stockbroker. The mother of three daughters, she lives with her family in Hillsborough, California, and divides her time between being a housewife, a writer, and a tournament bridge player. Of herself she says, "I enjoy music, books, kookie art, and people—most of all people." *Just Dial a Number* is Mrs. Maxwell's first novel. She has also written *Game of Truth*, an Archway Paperback, as well as short stories, mysteries, and children's plays.